D1622430

DEATH IN THE CARIBBEAN

DEATH IN
THE CARIBBEAN

by

J. R. L. ANDERSON

STEIN AND DAY/*Publishers*/New York

First published in the United States of America, 1977
Copyright © 1977 by J. R. L. Anderson
All Rights reserved
Printed in the United States of America
Stein and Day /*Publishers*/Scarborough House,
Briarcliff Manor, N.Y. 10510

Library of Congress Cataloging in Publication Data

Anderson, John Richard Lane, 1911–
Death in the Caribbean.

I. Title.
PZ4.A54755Das 1977 [PR6051.N3934] 823'.9'14 77-8748
ISBN 0-8128-2353-2

For Timothy

CONTENTS

AUTHOR'S NOTE

I wonder what would have happened if a Lady Macbeth had decided to pursue Shakespeare for libel? Or a Sir John Falstaff? Or a Mr Iago? Ruin for Shakespeare, I suppose. And (if imaginative literature has any value) some loss to the world. Accidental libel, the chance use of a fictitious name to which some real owner chooses to object, is the cruellest hazard to which an author is exposed. I am told that it offers no protection to say that one's characters have no real existence, that they are invented with the rest of one's story. Yet people in stories have to have names, and if they are to be credible they must be names drawn from the common stock of human nomenclature. For myself, apart from the financial risk, I should be deeply hurt if anyone tried to read himself or herself into a character of mine, for it would suggest laziness in my own imagination. So I do say that all the people in my tale, with the West Indian island in which it is set, are wholly and utterly imaginary. The sea, the trade wind, and the tropical bush are as real as I can make them, but the people who inhabit my story have precisely the same reality as the grin of the Cheshire Cat.

DEATH IN THE CARIBBEAN

I

EARTHQUAKE

"UNDER THE TABLE, I think," said our host. "At least it's good honest mahogany."

He slid, quite gracefully, from his chair at the end of the big table to crouch under its comfortingly solid top. I watched the wall of the house swaying and followed him. I like to think that I waited a fraction of a second for the woman sitting opposite to me to go first: perhaps I did, but the situation was so confused that I have no clear recollection of our order of precedence in taking cover. The dignified Negro butler, who had just replenished our glasses with rum punch, came too. Thoughtfully, he clutched the big silver bowl of punch as he crawled to shelter.

I had never before experienced an earthquake. This was quite different from a storm at sea. In a storm you know and feel your antagonist—wind and water can be killers, but they come at you in the open. This sick tremor that turned the stable world to a sort of jelly offered nothing you could even try to resist.

"The Carima River will be flowing uphill now, sir," the butler said.

I learned later that it is a popular belief that in Caribbean earthquakes the rivers reverse their flow. At the moment it didn't seem to matter much. From my position under the table the field of view was restricted, but it was enough to bring the sudden realisation that I was looking at the countryside where there should have been a solid wall. I saw a magnificent *poui* tree, a mass of golden flowers, bow its superb head and turn over, almost in slow motion. The next moment there was a horrible tortured scream of shattering timbers as the house fell on us. I found that I was holding the woman's hand, or she mine. The table shuddered as a mass of wreckage fell on it, but by some miracle of West Indian carpentry and the hard strength of mahogany, it did not collapse. It was as good a refuge as the

9

Morrison steel table shelters used in air raids during the Second World War.

Then there was a horrible smell of burning. "There can't be any more house to fall, and the place will be on fire. We must get out," our host said.

It wasn't easy. The table that saved us was more or less intact, but it was surrounded by a junkyard of broken woodwork and bits of furniture. Because it had been built of wood, there wasn't the choking mess of plaster dust that would have accompanied a house-fall in many parts of the world, but the house had stood for over a century, and there was dust enough. More dangerously, the inevitable fire that spreads from overturned cooking pots in kitchens was getting a savage hold on old, dry wood. Smoke filled our nostrils, and we could hear the dreadful crackle of flames getting nearer and nearer.

The butler got out first, quickly followed by our host. They heaved and tore at broken beams, and somehow cleared a way for us. The butler lifted out the woman as if she was a child, and our host gave a hand to me. "Run," he said, as soon as we were clear.

It was unnecessary advice—it was all that any of us wanted to do. Even so, the butler crawled back and salvaged the silver bowl before he started running. I glanced at my watch. It seemed unbelievable, but the whole disaster had taken place in rather less than four minutes.

The house stood—more accurately, had stood—on a gentle slope rising from the Carima River. Between the house and the river, the land, once bush, had long been gardens, and as soon as we were clear of the ruins of the building we were safe enough. The big trees that were going to fall, had fallen—there was nothing left to fall. Telling the woman to go down to the river bank and wait for us there, our host, the butler and I ran round the blazing ruins to the kitchen compound at the back, to see what help we could give to anyone who might be trapped. The compound, like the servants' quarters in most of the older West Indian houses, was single-storey, a row of rather flimsy low huts, roofed with coconut straw, grouped round three sides of a square. Their flimsy construction saved their occupants, and all seemed to have got out safely before the fire took hold. Satisfied that there was no one unaccounted for, we went back to the river. There was still some punch in the silver bowl. There were no glasses, and the butler solemnly handed the bowl to the woman to drink first.

"Good work, Adam," said our host. When the woman had had a drink, he took the bowl from her and handed it to the butler. "You next, Adam," he said. The butler tried to refuse, but our host insisted. After Adam had drunk he gave the bowl to me. Never has rum punch tasted better. I gave the bowl in turn to our host with the curious feeling that the four of us were sharing in some almost sacred rite. Perhaps we were. Human survival is, in a way, sacred, and is certainly the basis of much religious feeling.

When Sir Edmund Pusey said to me, "Peter, you need a holiday, and I've arranged just the thing for you, at the taxpayers' expense, too," I was naturally wary.

"Where do you want me to go?" I asked cautiously.

"To Nueva."

"And where is Nueva?"

"I don't believe you are as ignorant as all that. Nueva is the largest and least known of the Lesser Antilles. Next to Barbados, which was taken by the British in 1605, it is, or rather was, for it is independent now, the oldest British colony in the West Indies. It is somewhat off the main sailing routes, about 150 miles ENE of Dominica, and more nearly in the Atlantic than the other West Indian islands. You go there comfortably by air nowadays, and the island is exceptionally beautiful."

"If the place is independent, what is it to do with us?"

"Peter! I said I was sending you on holiday! Of course, there is a little job you might undertake in your spare time, as it were, when you're not swimming or drinking rum, to justify your expenses."

I felt still more alarmed. Sir Edmund is head of the Police Liaison Department at the Home Office, a powerful but little publicised arm of Government that acts partly as a kind of General Staff in the endless war against crime, partly as a co-ordinating body when the work of the police and the various defence and intelligence services is liable to overlap. I had been a regular officer in the Army—became, indeed, the youngest major in my regiment—but I left the Army when the regiment was amalgamated with two others, and there were three majors for every major's job. I went into industry and had another career as an up-and-coming tycoon. But that career, and with it my marriage, crashed when the firm of which I was general sales director was taken over by an even bigger concern. I had retired to what had been my father's cottage in South Devon, to lick my wounds and prove to myself that I could make a living with my hands as a carpenter when I got into Sir Edmund's clutches by becoming fortuitously involved in a curious case of drug-smuggling, in which, with my small boat which was my other passion in life, I was able to render some service to the police. After that he recruited me for a number of what he called his "little jobs", and finally had me recalled to the Army, promoted colonel, and seconded to his department as the representative of the armed services. Sir Edmund has many merits —imagination, high intelligence, and absolute loyalty to members of his staff. Against that, he is tiresomely ready to assume that you will always do whatever he wants done, and he is a little inclined to tell you half a story, reckoning that it is good for your soul, your wits, or something to work out the other half.

"Do you even know what the job is?" I asked coldly.

'Well, up to a point. But that's why I need you, Peter. You have a remarkable way of getting to the bottom of things."

'"Cut out the flattery. What is it this time?"

In another life, Sir Edmund would have made a good professor. He adopted what I call his lecturing posture, putting the tips of his fingers together, and looking beyond you rather than at you.

"You are quite right in holding that we have no business to interfere in the affairs of an independent former colony," he said. "But things are seldom as simple as they seem. The Nuevan Government still turns to us for technical assistance in all sorts of things, and the Nuevan economy is almost wholly dependent on loans and grants from the British taxpayer, and such other international aid as Her Majesty's Government can help the island to obtain. Nueva has no oil, or ashphalt, like Trinidad, no bauxite or banana industry, like Jamaica. Throughout its history the island has relied on one crop—sugar. Before the First World War, when beet sugar was virtually unknown, cane sugar was a reliable staple. It is very different nowadays—the world sugar market is a complex and bewildering affair. Nueva has a little cotton, the beautiful long-stapled West Indian cotton which

12

produces the finest cotton fabrics in the world. But cotton has been severely hit by competition from synthetic fibres. With the grants and loans it gets, the Nuevan Government is trying to develop a citrus fruit industry—the limes from its neighbour Dominica are world-famous—and, of course, it is doing everything it can to develop the tourist trade. Providing luxurious holidays for millionaires is not, however, the healthiest of economic activities for a native population most of whom are desperately poor.

"Nueva is cursed—or blessed, but sometimes such blessings take a long time to confer benefits—with a multi-racial society —Negro, East Indian and Chinese, with a handful of Europeans and a considerable community of mixed blood. In the mountainous interior there are even still a few indigenous Caribs, but they don't leave their mountains much. The island is quite big— about the size of Lincolnshire.

"The Negroes were brought originally from Africa as slaves. With the abolition of slavery the Negro population was understandably reluctant to continue working on the sugar estates, but these had to have labour. The problem was solved in nineteenth-century fashion by importing Chinese labourers under a system of indenture—so many years' work on the plantations after which they could, if they wished, be repatriated. When their indentured time was up, many of the Chinese preferred to stay on in Nueva. But not as labourers. Frugal, industrious, and often exceedingly able, the Chinese turned to shopkeeping and money-lending, building up big businesses—on a Nuevan scale —and not infrequently becoming the owners of plantations to whose masters they lent money on mortgage. That meant another problem of finding labour for the canefields. This time it was met by bringing in indentured labour from India. Like the Chinese, many of the East Indians—they are called East Indians to distinguish them from the native peoples of the West Indies, whose name perpetuates Columbus's error in believing that he had reached India—stayed on. Again, they did not stay on as labourers. They became the community's artisans and technicians, mechanics, brass-workers and silversmiths, and, a generation later, doctors, dentists and lawyers. Of course the divisions now between these various racial groups are not clear cut, but they retain a distinct racial entity which does not make for easy politics.

"The Prime Minister—unusual in the West Indies—is Chinese. He is called Mr Li Cook, and although the third generation of Nuevan-born Chinese he is pure Chinese: the Chinese and the East Indians have never gone in much for marriage outside their own communities. His curious mixture of a name is typical of the West Indian melting pot of peoples and languages—whether 'Cook' is a corruption of some Chinese name, or adopted from the name of some English planter whose estate the Li family took over, I don't know. He seems a good chap. He has just been in London for various negotiations with our Government, and in the course of his visit he came to see me."

Sir Edmund paused. I know a little Spanish, and said, "Isn't it rather ridiculous for an island—a country now, I suppose—to be called simply 'New'?"

The professorial manner was maintained. "It's just part of the historical muddle. The island is said to have been discovered by Columbus on his second voyage, though there is not much real evidence. Its original name was Nueva Rabida, called after a monastery at La Rabida, near Palos, where Columbus certainly stayed when he was making preparations for his first voyage from Palos. The 'Rabida' does rather suggest that Columbus gave the place its name. However, when the English got there 'Nueva Rabida' was too much for the lazy English tongue, and the 'Rabida' was soon dropped. It's been plain 'Nueva' ever since. There's a precedent for this. When I was in the Diplomatic Service I served briefly in Ethiopia. The name of the capital—Addis Ababa—means 'New Flowers' in Amharic. Most foreigners simply call it 'Addis'. If it's not your own language a place-name has no particular meaning except to denote a place."

"All right. I'm not going to alter the map. But why do you want me to go there?"

"Mr Li Cook is in trouble. He heads a fairly broad-based coalition, and as far as one can tell he is making a genuine effort to develop the Nuevan economy. The difficulties are appalling. He is aware of the dangers of over-dependence on tourists, but he has got to get foreign exchange from somewhere, and tourists are the quickest source of it. Moreover, although there's a coalition Government there are a couple of more extreme political parties outside it, and a vocal Opposition. They're all for a get-rich-quick policy, and in favour of selling off a large

14

part of the island's Atlantic coast to an American syndicate for development as a hotel and villa playground."

"Not our business."

"No . . . but it's not as simple as that. The Opposition seems to be an odd political mixture, keen on getting hold of American capital, but also standing for a kind of violent left-wing nationalism. In Mr Li's view, they only want American development so that at the appropriate moment they can stir up trouble and take over the lot."

"Again, not our business."

"Directly, of course not. But have a look at the map." He had an atlas on his desk, already opened on a general map of the North Atlantic. I went over to join him in studying it. He pointed to Nueva, a dot in the ocean. It was a dot, though, in a highly significant place, with nothing but sea between it and the British Isles, New York, and the Gibraltar entrance to the Mediterranean.

"A marvellous base for long-range submarines," Sir Edmund said reflectively. "It was not for nothing that the West Indies were fought over again and again when Britain, France and Spain were disputing for sea-power. Politically, the world may have changed—I doubt if it has changed much strategically. . . . You don't know this yet, but there is a special feature of the Atlantic coast of Nueva which makes it peculiarly suitable for a submarine base, the Chacarima caves. They are the deepest caves in the world, and they have never been fully explored. Many of the islands are volcanic. Nueva certainly is, and the caves are supposed to have been formed in some underground eruption in the geological past. The Carima river flows through them, emerging to reach the sea in a long, narrow bay, the Chacarima Inlet. This is all deep water, like a Norwegian fjord, and the deep water extends underground far inland through the caves. Fleets of submarines could lie up there, impervious to air attack, safe, perhaps, even from a nuclear bomb.

"The coast around the inlet is exceptionally beautiful, with long beaches of white sand. This is the area that the Opposition sees as the principal site of American tourist development."

"In American hands it would seem reasonably safe from being used for other purposes."

"If the Americans kept it, perhaps. The fear is that American money would be used for site engineering roadworks, harbour installations and the like, and then the whole development would be taken over."

"Can't the Prime Minister put a stop to anything of that sort?"

"Well, he can now.... What he can't do is to tell the Americans, whose money is needed to provide jobs for Nuevans, 'Don't come near the place because the next Government may chuck you out.' Somebody is presumably backing the Opposition, for they seem to have plenty of money. But it is unclear who is behind them. I was wondering if you could, perhaps, find out what is going on."

"What a holiday job! And who am I supposed to represent? I can't have any official status in Nueva."

"As a matter of fact, I've fixed that up for you already. The Nuevan Army—yes, there is a Nuevan Army—is thinking of equipping itself with the new British rifle. The Prime Minister, who sensibly doubles in the post of commander-in-chief, would be delighted to welcome the distinguished small-arms expert, Colonel Blair, as technical adviser in the use of the new rifle."

"I am not a small-arms expert."

"Damn it, you are a colonel, and are supposed to be able to fire a rifle. The Ministry of Defence is also delighted with the arrangement. The British taxpayer will be paying, anyway, and if some of the grants-in-aid to Nueva are spent on buying British rifles, at least a little of the money will come back to Britain."

"How have you sold me as a small-arms expert?"

"Well, the Ministry of Defence has some extremely able intelligence officers. I mention no names, but you are well enough aware of those who have reason to respect you in your—er—other capacities. It was not difficult for a word to be said in the right quarter. Anyway, Peter, there is a place booked for you on a British World Airways flight to Nueva tomorrow. Rosemary has all the papers for you. Have a word with her as you go out. Oh, and she's made an appointment for you at the Tropical Diseases Clinic for this afternoon, to make sure that your inoculations are all up to date."

That is Sir Edmund all over. What he offers with one hand, he has already taken from you with the other.

The flight to Nueva was as dull as most air-journeys are. By the time I got on the plane I was too exhausted to care. I have enough experience of life to know that things like tropical kit are best bought in the tropics, but I had to have some tropical uniform in order to appear respectable when I met the representatives of the Nuevan Army. However, it is wonderful what military tailors can do if you are really pressed, and in the intervals of getting jabbed at the Tropical Diseases Clinic and rushing to a chart agent to get some charts of Nueva and the Lesser Antilles I was fitted out with most of what I needed. Rosemary—she is Sir Edmund's secretary—had thoughtfully obtained two copies of the instruction manual for the new rifle, and although I had never fired the thing I reckoned that I could get by.

Normally I never drink outside the hours of noon to one-thirty or after six o'clock in the evening, but the plane took off at eight o'clock in the morning, and when a nice hostess brought round drinks at ten o'clock I was ready for a large whisky. "You are going to Nueva?" she said. "I'm afraid you will find whisky very expensive in Nueva—but they say that Nueva rum is the best in the world." This did not exactly comfort me, but it helped to make me feel a bit more resigned.

Nueva is a longish island, lying roughly north-west to south-east. The capital—Fort James—is on the southern, or Caribbean, coast, and most of the settlements are on that side of the island. We crossed the Atlantic coast too high to make out much of it, but the sea was an incredibly lovely blue, and I could just distinguish the famous white sand beaches. The mountainous interior of the island rises to some 6,000 feet, and we kept high as we flew over it. I didn't see much of Nueva until we began the descent to the airport outside Fort James, but then, tired as I was, the sheer beauty of the place was an excitement. There are no half-tones in the West Indian landscape—everything is in vivid primary colours, splashed on with the abandon of a happy child given free run of a paintbox. The blue of the sea is deep ultra-marine, the green of the bush-covered hills a pure Garden-of-Eden green, the red of the hibiscus flowers clear flame. There were other flowers whose names I did not then know, notably the brilliant yellow of a forest-tree called, I learned later, *poui*, and another magnificent flowering tree called Flame of the Forest.

I was met at the airport by a brigadier of the Nuevan Rifles, commanding a small guard of honour who presented arms with the snap of a Guards unit. After inspecting the guard, the brigadier took me in a staff car to the Fort James Hotel, where I had not merely a room but a suite, overlooking some gardens with a pond full of lovely water lilies. The brigadier invited me to dine with him that evening, saying that a car would be sent to collect me in an hour, to give me time to have a bath. He also gave me a note from the Prime Minister, inviting me to call on him in the morning.

I quite enjoyed that evening. We dined privately in the brigadier's house, a few miles outside Fort James, and it was my first experience of the West Indian fruit. I have had mangoes in India, but they were poor things beside the magnificent fruit that grow in Nueva.

The brigadier impressed me. He was youngish, not much over forty, and of pure Negro blood. He had joined the Army in the last days of colonial rule, had won quick promotion, and had been to our own Staff College. He was highly educated, and I felt that if the Nuevans could produce many officers of his type there could be nothing much wrong with their Army. That, I reflected, was perhaps part of the problem: if tempted to play politics, an efficient Army is in a strong position to do more or less what it likes in a new state. I did not know where the Army's political sympathies lay, and the brigadier did not enlighten me. He said nothing to indicate that he knew of the non small-arms training side of my mission, and of course I was careful to be no more than a Regular British Officer, keen to see that the Nuevans got the best of what we could provide.

We did not wholly avoid politics, but discussed them only in the most general terms. I was naturally interested to learn how Nueva was making out in independence, and the brigadier was ready enough to discuss his country's economic problems. "I am not in the least hostile to the British," he said. "Indeed, I did rather well out of your old Empire. I was a clever boy, went to a church school, and won a scholarship that took me to a university in Canada. Your Army taught me a lot, and treated me well. As I have met your people, I have no complaints. But that's the point—*as I have met them.* If I lived in shanty-town on the other side of Fort James, if I had no job and not much prospect of ever having one, I couldn't feel as well-disposed to the people who—from my point of view—created the mess I have to live in. I don't think the British were ever particularly brutal masters—certainly far less brutal than some of the other colonial powers. You sent us good administrators, gave us, on the whole, good schools. Your law, again on the whole, was good law, deserving our respect—we have not changed the civil and criminal law you left us. Broadly, my complaint against the old colonial administration is that it saw no future for us. Bright individuals who could be assimilated to your own society—Fine, you said, come in! To the rest of the population you were polite, reasonably kind, and completely careless. You didn't particularly want Nuevan industry—you preferred that we should import your products. You wanted our raw materials, sugar, chiefly, a little cotton, a little cocoa, but you wanted them for your own factories, you didn't want them processed here. And if your factories found that they could get cheaper sugar, cheaper cocoa, somewhere else—well, that was just too bad for Nueva. You see, we have to start from where you left off, and you never really took us very far."

I couldn't help feeling that he was largely right. "I wonder if any empires have done much better for their subject people—Rome, Spain, for instance," I said.

"Probably not. In a way, a woolly sort of way, if you will forgive my saying so, I think the old British Empire was perhaps the most well-meaning of the lot. What you must understand is that it isn't very nice to be a subject person. One thing you have given us that I think our grandchildren and great-grandchildren may even bless you for—and that's the English language."

"It's good of you to say so. Maybe we can also give you, or at least sell you, a good rifle, too," I said.

He laughed. "We shall get on well together, Colonel. I understand you are seeing the Prime Minister in the morning—I shall send a car to your hotel to take you to him. Tomorrow evening the Defence Staff has arranged a small reception for you. After that we can get down to business. You will find that our chaps can shoot quite straight."

I wondered what he meant by that.

II

THE CAVALS

ONE IS NOT at one's best on emerging from an earthquake. I have tried to explain what brought me to Nueva, but the events of those days are still rather confused in my mind. Surveying the ruins of Edward Caval's once-beautiful house it struck me as among the wilder lunacies of life that I had been sent to him by the Prime Minister to try to learn if he really wanted to sell his share of the Caval estate to an American syndicate. Well, earthquakes have an effect on property values, perhaps.

My visit, although it had secondary intentions, was, on the face of things, purely social. I had been three days in Nueva, and you can't be three hours in Nueva without hearing the name Caval. Mr Li Cook told me about him at our first meeting.

The Prime Minister lived in what had been Government House, formerly the Colonial Governor's official residence in Fort James. He received me in his private quarters, without a touch of formality. A secretary brought me in, but she was at once dismissed, and we were alone together. The room was on the ground floor, opening through a loose hanging screen of *cus-cus* grass—wetted, it gives off a scent of eau de cologne—on to a delightful garden. "Come into the garden," he said, as soon as we had shaken hands. Outside, he went on, "We will talk, if you don't mind, in the garden—it will be cool enough under the trees they call *las madres de cacao*, 'the mothers of the cocoa'. They are forest trees, grown on our cocoa plantations to shade the cocoa crop. They are beautiful trees, and will shade us just as well as they do cocoa."

The trees were a good hundred yards from the house. In their shelter the Prime Minister explained, "It is not that I am naturally distrustful, but in these days of high technology, it is as well to take no chances. *Las madres de cacao* will keep their secrets—I am less sure of walls and furniture. How did you get on with the brigadier?"

"Quite well, I think. He gave me a nice dinner, and he was interesting to talk to. He is very intelligent."

"Yes, he is certainly that. He might even be on my side... he is a Nuevan patriot, I think. He knows nothing of the—er—inner reasons for your visit. At least, I have told him nothing, though he may have his own sources of intelligence."

"He gave no indication of being concerned with anything but the new rifle."

"Good. That is quite genuine—I think we should equip our forces with it. I must leave you to get on with that side of the business in your own way. I want to talk to you this morning about the Cavals. You have heard of the Caval family?"

"I noticed Caval Street in Fort James, and I think the brochure about the hotel in my bedroom had something about a Caval being the proprietor."

"Of course. The Cavals used to own most of Nueva, they are still by far our richest family. The first Edward Caval—the first, at any rate, to have anything to do with our own history, was an Oxfordshire squire who supported Charles I in the English Civil War, and lost all his possessions as a result. After the restoration, Charles II gave him Nueva as a reward. The King certainly never set eyes on the place, though possibly Prince Rupert did. But it was a cheap way of paying debts. The first Edward Caval ran the island like a private estate, as, I suppose, it was. He left two sons, another Edward—there is always an Edward Caval—and another son, Antoine, by a French mistress. There was bad blood between the half-brothers. Edward, as the legitimate heir, felt that the whole island should be his, but his father had been fond of Antoine's mother and apparently liked the boy himself. Anyway, he left a perfectly good will, giving Antoine nearly half the island. Edward tried to challenge the will in the English courts, but after a law suit that dragged on for years, the will was upheld. The result was a kind of private war in Nueva, each brother arming his slaves and trying to take the other's land by force. Things got so bad that the English Government sent a naval force to intervene. Edward was killed, and the administration was formally taken over by the Crown, who sent out a Governor and gave him a military garrison to maintain order. This gave the island a recognised Government, but it made no difference to proprietorship. Edward left a son who succeeded to his plantations, and Antoine kept his. The two families adopted a policy of live and let live, disliking each other, but combining whenever they wanted to defeat some piece of colonial legislation they didn't like. Enjoying most of the economic power in the island, they generally won.

"But all this is fairly ancient history, though it is necessary to give you an understanding of the background to our present situation. The Edward Cavals have kept their land, and—unlike most planter families, who made enormous fortunes out of sugar in the eighteenth century, and bought country estates in England rather than put money back into Nueva—they have been excellent landlords. The Antoine Caval line was more given to extravagant living, and in the course of time lost much of their land. They still have some, though, on the Caribbean coast of Nueva. Most of the Atlantic coast belongs to the present Edward. He is a widower, without children, and it is far from clear what the sucession is.

"The present head of the Antoine Caval branch of the family, one Nicolas Caval, is politically inclined, and supports the Opposition leader, Nelson Ebenezer, in pressing for rapid American development of a tourist industry on our Atlantic coast. The land, however, belongs to Edward.

"You must understand, Colonel, that we were *given* independence—we did not obtain it for ourselves by revolution. That explains, at least to some extent, why we have not upset existing law, and have not interfered much with established ownership in the island. We are a sovereign Government, of course, and doubtless we could expropriate the Caval lands, but I am not myself greatly in favour of such action. And, as I said, Edward Caval continues his branch of the family's tradition of being good landlords. His estates are the best run and most profitable on the island, and he is popular with the workers on them. I do not want revolutionary change—seldom, I think, does it do much to improve the human lot. Confucius is politically out of fashion, but his teachings which, in a sense, I have inherited, embody much wisdom. Reform certainly—my Government has already promoted many useful reforms, and if we are given the chance we shall achieve much more. But revolution, no."

He paused, and said nothing more while we walked to the end of the avenue under the Mothers of the Cocoa trees, turned, and came back. I found myself liking Mr Li Cook, and wondering what chance a man of his moderation had of staying in power.

When we had completed one turn of our walk in silence, he went on, "If Edward Caval were to sell out to the Americans there is little I could do to prevent vast development of our Atlantic coast, with consequences no one can foresee. But is he willing to sell? It would be against the whole Caval tradition, but he has no child to follow him, and he may have lost heart. There is another possibility—Caval dynastic feeling may be so strong that he will leave his estates to the Nicolas Cavals, who would almost certainly want to sell. I am hoping, Colonel, that perhaps you can find out for me." He ended almost wistfully.

Put like that, it seemed a ridiculous proposition. It was no part of my job as an agent of the British Government to meddle with the problems of land ownership in an independent ex-Crown Colony. But I thought of Nueva's position on the globe—in certain circumstances control of its Atlantic coast might be of vital concern to Britain and her allies. The Prime Minister at least seemed to be on our side. I wasn't being asked to act in any way—I was merely being asked to help in finding out some facts. Practically, though, could I be of any help? Why couldn't the Prime Minister ask Edward Caval? Well, I could see that there might be reasons why he did not want to seem too interested. If I could meet the Caval man, it was possible that I might be able to talk to him. I didn't rate the chances of learning anything important as being very high, but having come to Nueva I might as well have a go. I said that I thought I understood the position, and would do what I could to help, though the Prime Minister must recognise that I might easily achieve nothing.

"Of course," he said. "But isn't all life something of a gamble? I will arrange for you to meet Edward Caval. Let's see— tomorrow, I think, you had better devote yourself to the Army. The day after tomorrow—yes, it is reasonable for you to have a rest after a strenuous day on parade. I'll get Edward Caval to invite you to breakfast."

"Breakfast?" I was a little startled.

He laughed. "You must learn to speak Nuevan English. Our breakfast is what you call your lunch, though it is usually a little earlier, around eleven-thirty to noon. Our day begins early, you see, and we follow the hot-country habit of starting with no more than a cup of coffee and some fruit. The shops are all open by seven, and all Government offices by eight. Nothing much happens between eleven-thirty and four o'clock in the afternoon—it is a time for breakfast, and going to sleep.... Edward Caval takes no part in politics, but he likes to regard himself as our leading citizen, as, in a sense, he is. When we have a distinguished visitor I generally get Edward Caval to invite him to his house at Chacarima—he rather likes to be asked. Some time tomorrow there will be a note at your hotel inviting you to breakfast at Chacarima. You will enjoy the drive—it is no more than fifty miles or so, through some of our most spectacular countryside. I'll send a car to pick you up at nine, which will allow ample time for the drive."

The Prime Minister could certainly get things done. There duly was a polite note from Edward Caval, delivered to the hotel by hand. But first—my day with the Army.

That really began on the evening of my talk with the Prime Minister, when I attended a reception given for me by the Chief of Staff. He was a certain General Henriques, of mixed Portuguese and Negro ancestry, the senior officer present, though I did not think him as impressive a personality as my Brigadier Moses Ezra—such biblical names are rather a feature of the Negro community in Nueva, particularly in families which have been socially well established for two or three generations. It was a friendly gathering, and the general gave me the recipe for the famous Nuevan rum punch:

> *One of sour*
> *Two of sweet*
> *Three of strong*
> *And four of weak*

This, he explained, meant one measure of lime juice, two measures of sugar, three measures of rum and four of water. Nuevan rum, I should add, is about 90 degrees proof.

The work began at seven next morning, when I took a parade of a company of the 1st Nuevan Rifles which had been equipped with the new British rifle. They were a smart lot, and we marched off to the butts to put the rifle through its paces. To my alarm, I found that I was expected to fire first—with an audience of Staff officers and keen young riflemen.

24

In my proper Army days I had at least been an infantry officer, and at one time I was a fair shot, representing my battalion at Bisley a couple of times. Providence was on my side that morning. We were to fire at 300 yards, at a target that would come up for five seconds. I had never even seen, let alone fired, the new rifle before, but (thanks to Rosemary) I had studied the instruction manual, and understood more or less how the thing worked. It had a good feel to it, and balanced sweetly. Deciding that there was nothing to be gained by dragging out things, and that my best chance was to let my old training work as automatically as possible, I got down quickly and as soon as the target came up sent off five rounds. Brigadier Ezra and his mates were watching the target through field glasses. I heard a sort of collective gasp of astonishment, and supposed that I had contrived to miss the bloody thing altogether. But no. A runner was sent to bring back the target, and when it came I saw that there was one bullet hole almost dead centre. Closer inspection showed that the top edge of the hole was slightly nicked as if another bullet had gone through it. Where the other three rounds went I had no idea, and fortunately no one else had. They assumed that all five rounds had gone through the same hole. "I have seen good shooting in my time, but nothing like this," said the brigadier. "I really must congratulate you, Colonel—both on your shooting and on the rifle."

After that I could do nothing wrong. The brigadier and the other officers all tried out the rifle, and then the riflemen had a go, in various combinations of single shots and rapid automatic fire. With my heart in my mouth and the instruction manual vividly in my mind I then gave a demonstration of stripping the rifle, and mercifully succeeded in getting it together again. "There is no doubt that we need this weapon," the brigadier said. "Even without the Colonel's demonstration I thought it a good rifle—now I am convinced that it is the finest infantry rifle in the world. How soon can you let us have it in quantity?"

I said that I should have to report back to the Ministry at home, but I was confident that an order to re-equip the Nuevan Army would be given the highest priority. I also offered to arrange for a group of NCO instructors to be sent out, to help with initial training. We then adjourned for the Neuvan breakfast, and (at least as far as I was concerned) some much-needed Nuevan rum punch.

The brigadier drove me back to my hotel, and on the way he said, "I've had a note from the Prime Minister's office to say that he has arranged for you to spend tomorrow sightseeing. I am glad that you will have an opportunity of seeing a little of our country. I will keep in touch with you through the Prime Minister's office. When you get back to Fort James I'd be most grateful if you would give a lecture to our Staff course on modern infantry tactics in the use of small arms."

I said I'd be glad to, and the rest of the day was my own. After allowing for the Nuevan siesta, I called on the British High Commissioner, whom I'd met at the reception last night, and gave him an account of our apparent success in selling the rifle to the Nuevan Army. He was pleased, and sent a message for me to the Ministry of Defence. He also invited me to dinner, and I spent a pleasant evening with him and his wife. I told him that I'd been invited to visit Mr Edward Caval next day, and he was pleased about that, too. "It's quite a compliment," he said. "It means that the Nuevans are really giving you VIP treatment. Edward Caval is a bit of an odd fish, but I must say that if all West Indian planters had been more like him history might have turned out differently. He's played very straight with the Nuevans since independence—partly self-interest, perhaps, for he's got a lot to lose. But he's useful to the Nuevans, too—as a sort of historical monument, a cross between an archbishop and an ex-king who keeps right out of politics. They only use him, though, for people they really want to impress, so it looks as if you've made quite a hit. Caval has the most wonderful old butler, quite out of this world. You'll enjoy meeting him."

I did. The Caval house seemed to have about five miles of drive, winding from a bridge over the Carima river through beautiful, park-like country. The river also turned below the bridge, so that when we got to the house it was flowing round the low hillock on which the house stood, making a perfect landscape setting. The butler met the car as it drew up outside the house, opened the door for me, and said in a voice that would have done credit to the butler of an Oxford college, "Mr Caval has asked me to say that we are proud to welcome Colonel Blair to Chacarima." Then he said to the driver, "The colonel will be here for most of the day, so please do not wait for him. There is breakfast for you in the housekeeper's room. Please suit yourself

26

about returning to Fort James. We will get the colonel back when he wishes to leave."

He directed the driver where to go for his meal, and then he showed me into the house, or rather, to a comfortable chair on a wide verandah overlooking the river. "Mr Caval will be with you in a moment, sir," he said.

I had barely time to take in the view from the verandah when the butler was back, with an elderly man, white-haired, thin, but without a trace of stoop, and with a much younger woman, "Mr Caval and Mrs Ruth Caval for Colonel Blair," he said formally, and withdrew.

Caval held out his hand. "I'm delighted to see you, Colonel," he said. "It is very good of you to come all this way to visit an old man, but I daresay the Prime Minister has given you his version of Caval history. Let me introduce Ruth, who is staying with me. She is the wife of a member of another branch of the Caval family, who is at present in the United States. It is a distant relationship, but nonetheless real."

I had heard nothing of any Ruth Caval. If she was married to a Caval she was presumably not a Caval herself, and I wondered where she fitted in. She was distinctly attractive, dark haired, with the very clear skin that sometimes goes with dark hair, and intelligent, lively eyes. I put her down as still in her twenties, but I learned later that she was thirty-one.

The introductions over, the butler returned with drinks on a silver tray. "I hope you will sample our Chacarima punch later," Edward Caval said. "After the drive from Fort James I thought that you might be better sustained by a glass of our oldest rum itself—it has been matured for over half a century." He handed me a glass, and took one himself. Mrs Caval had a tall glass of iced lime-juice. The rum was exceptionally pale, as pale as fine old brandy. It was also delicious, though I realised as soon as I tasted it that it was not a drink to be trifled with.

"Your health, Colonel," Caval said. "This rum was laid down by my grandfather, distilled, of course, from our own cane. It is rather moving, I think, that a man long in his grave should be able still to provide for his family's guests. I have replaced what I have drawn from the stocks left by my forbears, but who will drink my rum half a century from now I do not know. Times change, but whether for better or worse, again I do not know."

Mrs Caval asked about my home in England. "It seems a pity you couldn't bring your wife," she said.

"It would have been difficult, because I haven't got a wife. As for my home, well, yes, I have a cottage near Salcombe in South Devon, but I don't often see it nowadays. My job is based on London and I have chambers in the Temple. I contemplate retirement more and more frequently, but something always seems to get in the way."

"You're not nearly old enough to retire."

"Thank you for the compliment. But I don't know what is old enough. I like sailing my little Salcombe yawl, and I like working with my hands at making furniture. I think most of us arrange our lives pretty badly—by the time we do retire there's not enough life left to do the things we really want to do."

"But I expect you really want to do your Service job," Mr Caval broke in. "When the Prime Minister telephoned about you he said that you were a defence adviser, but he wasn't very explicit. What brings you to Nueva? I'm sorry, perhaps I shouldn't have asked that."

"I don't think there is any particular secret about my visit. The British Army has recently developed a new rifle, which a number of Allied armies are thinking of adopting. We have no formal alliance with Nueva, but it seems unthinkable that we should ever be engaged in hostilities, and we are always ready to offer technical help. The Nuevan Army is interested in our rifle, and I was invited to come out to demonstrate it. We had, I think, a fairly satisfactory demonstration yesterday—at any rate, the Nuevan Chiefs of Staff seemed pleased. Today, I understand—and thanks to you—is my reward."

We talked lightly of this and that until the butler came to tell us that breakfast—which I should have called lunch—was served. We had just started the first course when the earthquake happened.

Mr Caval surveyed the ruins of his house with what seemed to me remarkable detachment. "Once these old wooden houses catch fire there is nothing to be done," he said. "It may be worth searching the wreckage later to see what, if anything, has survived. But Adam will see to that. I have several other houses, so my own loss is not all that great. But Ruth has lost all her clothes, and neither of you has had breakfast. We must find out how extensive the earthquake has been. Our telephone here will be out of action, but the estate office is across the river, and it is possible that the line there will still be working. We get minor shocks from time to time, but I have never known one on the other side of the river. Here we are apparently on some fault related geologically to the Chacarima caves—I had hoped to show you the caves, Colonel, but that must now wait. The last serious shock was in my grandfather's time, when the house was damaged, but not destroyed. Can you walk about a mile and a half? We do not need to go back to the bridge—we are quite near the boathouse, and we can cross the river by boat. Let us go to the estate office, and see if the shock has affected Fort James. If not, I shall send you both to the hotel there, in time, I hope, for Ruth to go shopping. The hotel belongs to me."

"I'm staying there already," I said.

"Then you shall return as my guest. You will be company for Ruth until I can get things sorted out."

The boathouse was damaged and leaning drunkenly over the river, but it was a flimsy structure of bamboo and palm thatch, and it had not totally collapsed. A punt moored under it was still servicable, though it was half full of water. There were some calabashes, used as balers, still in the boathouse, and Mr Caval and the butler baled while I tackled the wreckage to get the boat out. When we were ready to embark Mr Caval sent Adam back to the ruins of the house. "You must arrange new homes for the servants," he said. "I shall probably go to Naurataka House, about twenty miles up the coast—with luck, that will not have been affected. Most of the staff may like to go there, too, but we must meet their wishes in every way we can. They will need money, Adam, for all will have lost possessions. You must see to that for me. If the estate office is undamaged, I shall send cars from there."

The butler bowed, and went off. Mr Caval, Ruth Caval and I got into the punt, and I paddled it about seventy-five yards to the other bank. There was a little landing stage which seemed intact. We secured the punt, and walked up a path through lime trees.

The estate office was a substantial group of buildings, forming a compound round a big sugar-mill. Everything seemed undamaged, but the smoke of the fire from Chacarima House had been seen, and knots of people were standing around anxiously. As we approached there was a sort of cheer, and an Indian dressed in spotless white drill came running up to us. "You are safe, then, Mr Caval. Thank God, thank God," he said.

"This is Mr Ram Das, my manager," Caval said. "Thank you, Ram Das. The house, I fear, is destroyed, but nobody is hurt."

"What happened, sir?"

"What happened! There was a severe earthquake, which brought down the house, and it was set alight by overturned fires in the kitchens."

Mr Ram Das looked astonished. "We felt nothing here, no tremor at all."

"Is the telephone still working?"

"Of course, sir."

"Then telephone the manager at the Fort James hotel. Ask if everything is all right there, and if it is say that Mrs Ruth Caval and my guest Colonel Blair are on their way, and that I wish them to have the best rooms in the hotel."

"At once, sir."

Mr Ram Das came back in a few minutes, looking even more puzzled. "No one felt any earthquake in Fort James," he said. "Everything is completely normal. The manager is most distressed to learn of your loss. And of course he is seeing to your instructions."

"Good. Now I want a car to take Mrs Ruth Caval and Colonel Blair to Fort James, and I want two lorries and another car for Chacarima. I shall stay here with you for a bit. Ruth, you will have a good deal of shopping to do, and I think you'd better go off with Colonel Blair forthwith—if you can wait to eat until you get to Fort James."

"Of course I can wait. But what about you?"

"Don't worry about me. Ram Das will look after me, and I want to see to the evacuation of the staff to Naurataka. I shall telephone you this evening to let you know what is happening. Oh, and you will need money. Ram Das, can you get me a sheet of notepaper, please?" When this was brought he wrote a note and gave it to Ruth Caval. "Give this to the manager at the hotel," he said. "You can call on him for whatever you need in the way of cash."

Ruth Caval said nothing at all for nearly twenty miles of our drive. She'd had a savage shock, and I didn't try to make conversation. The country through which we drove seemed quite unharmed. It had been an extraordinarily limited earthquake.

When Ruth Caval did speak, she said, "Colonel Blair, do you believe that you can predict an earthquake?"

It was an odd question, and I didn't answer at once. "We've had a strange introduction, but I feel that fellow-survivors of an earthquake should be on Christian name terms. The name's Peter."

She gave a nervous little laugh, but I felt that the tension she was under was slightly relaxed. "All right, Peter and Ruth— quite biblical," she said. "But you haven't answered my question."

"I don't know how to answer it because I don't know anything about earthquakes. I've never heard that seismologists have had much success in predicting them. In Japan, where earthquakes are a serious concern, I believe they put more faith in soothsayers, and the shape of clouds. But why do you ask?"

"Because our earthquake was predicted. It was predicted before I left New York, nearly a month ago."

"Who predicted it?"

"That doesn't matter now. The point is, is it possible?"

"Offhand, I should have thought it exceedingly unlikely."

"Yes, but it happened. Look, Peter, you don't know anything about me, but I'm a mathematician—at least, I'm a university lecturer in maths. I'm not an expert in earthquakes, but I know something about probability. And the number of variables that must occur to produce an earthquake must be so great that I don't see how you can predict one a month ahead, and for one particular small area of the earth's surface."

"You can guess, I suppose. The wildest guesses have come off sometimes."

"Was this just a guess? I don't know, I don't know." She was speaking almost to herself.

It struck me as a fairly mad conversation, and I put it down to the strain she was obviously suffering. It also struck me as a rather unhealthy line of talk, and I thought I'd try to change the subject.

"Are you staying long in Nueva?" I asked.

"A week, a month, for ever ... God knows."

That didn't seem much better. "Look, Ruth, you seem to be suffering from a kind of delayed earthquake shock, if there is such a thing," I said. "Whatever it is you've had a bad time

31

We can discuss the prediction of earthquakes and anything else you like later. But we're going to be in Fort James in less than an hour, and it's time you considered toothbrushes."

She laughed—a better laugh this time. "Sorry. You're rather a dear. And you're quite right—I've never been quite as destitute as this before. I've got nothing but what I'm wearing—even my handbag went. It's hard to know where to begin."

"A toothbrush is a good starting point. But we can be more scientific, mathematical, if you like. Let's start with suitcases, to carry the things you're going to buy, and then work out what you're going to put in them. I've got a notebook. You can make a list."

I handed her my notebook and a pencil, but she said, "I'm no good at writing in cars. I'll think of things, and you can write them down."

I duly wrote "Suitcases", and she began, "Toothbrush, nail-file, clothes, I suppose . . . but what clothes? Oh, just put clothes, and I'll walk round the shop and buy something. And shoes, of course. And a fountain pen. And I wonder if I could get a copy of *Alice Through the Looking Glass*, and Bertrand Russell's *History of Western Philosophy*—I must have something to read. I'm afraid I'm not being very systematic. It's really awfully difficult."

Nevertheless, it helped. I thought of one or two practical things like handkerchiefs, scissors, a packet of needles and a reel of thread. "Though I could lend you my sailmaker's kit," I said.

"Sailmaker's kit?"

"Yes, it's a yachtsman's kit, in a small canvas wallet. I always travel with it—I find a sailmaker's palm a great deal easier to use than a thimble. And if you sew on a button with waxed twine, it doesn't come off again. Mind you, it's a slightly extended kit now, with some ordinary needles and bits of wool for darning, as well."

"No wonder you don't need a wife! I'm not sure, though, if any normal woman could live with a sailmaker's kit."

She was more cheerful now, and by the time we got to the hotel was chatting away almost happily. The manager came out to meet us. "We need," I said, "two of the largest glasses of rum punch that you've got. Then we need something to eat— not an elaborate meal, but I wonder if you could produce an omelette? Then Mrs Caval will need a car to go shopping."

"It shall all be arranged. Will you go up to your rooms first?"

"We'll have the rum first, I think. We need it."

"Of course, sir. Mrs Caval's suite has a private sitting-room. Will you have your meal there?"

"Of course."

We had our drinks on the verandah of the hotel. The manager wanted to move me to a larger suite, saying that Mr Caval had instructed him to offer it to me, but I said that I was quite happy where I was. The next thing was that Brigadier Ezra drove up. "I have heard of the disaster," he said. "Thank God you are all right."

I introduced him to Mrs Caval. "She was staying at Chacarima, and she has lost all her clothes, and everything she had with her," I explained. "I have promised Mr Caval to look after her. You will understand that it's going to be a busy afternoon."

"Indeed. And you must get some rest too, Colonel. Let me know at once if there is anything I can do to help. I came only to offer my services."

"It is extraordinarily good of you."

Then I was called to the telephone. It was the Prime Minister's office, and in a moment I was put through to the Prime Minister himself. He expressed great concern, and added, "There are no reports of any damage outside Chacarima."

"It was a mercifully limited earthquake," I said.

"They are not unknown, particularly in that part of Nueva, but they seldom do much damage. I am most distressed that this should have been your introduction to our distinguished citizen."

"It was an interesting introduction, anyway. I shall certainly meet Mr Caval again. I liked him very much." The Prime Minister, I thought, could make what he liked of that.

By the time all this was over our meal was ready in Ruth's suite. It was certainly palatial—virtually a whole wing of the hotel, on the ground floor, and opening on to a private garden. "Have you finished hobnobbing with the Government?" she asked.

"I hope so."

"Well, you seem to have taken me over. I think I'm grateful, but I'm not quite sure."

III

NAURATAKA

THAT HORRIBLE AFTERNOON came to an end. When she got around to organising herself, Ruth Caval was efficient, and in three hours she restored wardrobe, toiletries and footwear. Fort James could not provide Bertrand Russell—I was surprised, and rather pleased, at the amount of time she gave to hunting for him—but it did produce a copy of *Alice*, and also a modern reprint of Waterton's *Wanderings in South America*, which, I told her, would make good bedside reading for a mathematician. (Later she asked why I thought so, and I explained that it showed a world that had nothing to do with maths.)

While she was unpacking, Edward Caval telephoned, and after speaking to her he was put through to me. I was having a bath, but with that curious blend of the modern and the medieval that is (sometimes) one of the charms of the Caribbean, there was a telephone in the bathroom. After inquiring how we were, he said that he was installed at Naurataka, and that he would like me to come back with Ruth and stay for a few days. "It is, I think, beyond the local earthquake belt," he added. I said that I should be delighted to revisit him.

In clean clothes, and feeling more than ready for a drink, I called on Ruth. I found her looking forlorn, and reading *Alice*.

"Cheer up," I said, "most women would enjoy all those new clothes."

"Well, I'm not most women."

"I wondered if you'd let me take you out to dinner."

"Haven't you had enough of me?"

I considered this. "What are the alternatives?" I asked.

"The hotel serves quite good food. And I've got *Alice*, and that other book you wished on me."

"And for me?"

"A single man can always find plenty of entertainment."

"My dear Ruth, you are rather an ass. Do you know many people in Fort James?"

"I don't know anybody at all. I come from New York."

"I come from South Devon, which is even farther from Nueva than New York. So we're in the same boat, more or less."

"All right. Where shall we go?"

"There's a booklet of the delights of Nueva in my room. It says there's a beach about ten miles out of Fort James, with a waterfront restaurant and hibiscus leaning over the tables. We might find a table where the hibiscus didn't get into the soup."

Anata Beach turned out to be a charming place. The restaurant really was on the beach, in a clearing where trees came almost to the water's edge. I can't vouch for the hibiscus because night comes early in the tropics and it was dark when we got there, but there was a bonus that I hadn't expected—fireflies. They weren't round the tables, because the tables had electric light, but the place was well-planned, with low-powered lighting, and the rim of darkness round the trees sparkled with the jewel-glints of fireflies. Ruth was a bit edgy during dinner, making brittle, rather forced, conversation, but as we sat over coffee she seemed suddenly to relax. "I'm sorry, Peter," she said. "I've been horrid to you, and you have been very nice to me. Are you the sort of person I can talk to?"

"I'm a great deal older than you are," I replied, a little guardedly. "I can't claim any particular wisdom, but I am, or was, a soldier, and the Army tries to keep its head."

"Well, I don't know what to do. You see, I'm not married to any Caval."

"Does Mr Caval think you are?"

"I don't know. I don't see how he can—but I don't know him at all well. No, it's not like that. I'm quite properly Mrs Caval, at least I suppose I am if I want to be, but I don't, much. You see, I was married to Charles Caval, but we were divorced about a year ago. Do you know anything about Caval history?"

"I know a sort of guide-book version of it, about the quarrels between the two seventeenth-century half-brothers, and all that."

"It's true enough, at least as true as family history ever is, though Charles told me so many lies when I was married to him that I don't know what to believe about any Cavals. But that's a bit beside the point. Charles is the son of Nicolas Caval, that's the other branch of the Cavals, supposed to be the bitter enemies of Edward Caval's lot. Anyway, I met him just after I'd taken my D.Phil. I'd been working very hard, and I went on vacation to Florida. Charles was on vacation, too—he's a physicist, and a very able one, or he could be if he stuck at anything. I didn't know anything about Nueva then. We had a hectic love affair, got married in the States, and went to live at the university where Charles had a research job. Things went wrong from the start. I was all dewy-eyed and romantic then, I suppose, and I began by respecting Charles, and I saw him as a Professor of Physics one day. We'd not been back a week when I found that he was sleeping with one of the lab. assistants, and she was only one of a string. The other campus wives tried to be very sweet and wanted to pity me—you don't know how vile women can be when they want to pity another woman. I stood it for a bit— you see, I respected Charles as a scientist until I discovered that he was bone-idle and not above pinching the results of one of his own students' research. The boy came to me about it, in great distress. Then I had to get out. I brushed up my D.Phil and got a job in a mid-west municipal college—there's rather a shortage of good maths teachers, and I am good. I've got a better job now, but that's by the way.

"Charles didn't care two cents about my leaving him. I didn't ask for any money, and he never offered to send me anything— he never has. I had a bad time, because my parents are dead, and I've never had any money apart from what I've earned in student jobs. But I managed. Then some laywer wrote to say that Charles wanted a divorce. That seemed to tidy up the situation, and I was really thankful to get the whole business of my marriage over and done with. I never saw Charles again after I left, and for a long time I'd quite stopped thinking of him. I was still called Caval, because that was the name I'd applied for my first job in, and it just went on. It didn't seem to matter, anyway.

"Then I got a letter from Edward Caval. How he got hold of my address in New York I don't know, but he did somehow. It was rather a touching letter—kind of eighteenth-century good manners. But you've met Edward Caval, and you'll know what I mean. I can't show you the letter because it went up with the rest of my things at Chacarima, but I can remember it almost word for word. It began 'My dear Ruth, (if I may call you so),'

36

and went on, 'I am an old man, and, as you may know, my branch of the Caval family will die with me. I have a great wish to meet one of your generation who bears the name Caval, and I am wondering if you would do me the honour of visiting me at Chacarima. I enclose a return air ticket from New York to Nueva. You will see that it is undated—all you have to do is to make a reservation with the air line, and let me know the date on which, as I hope, you can come. I shall then arrange for a car to meet you at Fort James airport.' He didn't even mention Charles.

"Well, I wasn't all that keen on having anything to do with any more Cavals, but Edward seemed about the best of the bunch. I'd heard of him from Charles—of course, he never had a good word to say for Edward, but I'd learned to regard the reciprocal of anything Charles said as probably coming somewhere near the truth, so I was slightly disposed to think well of Edward. And I did need a vacation, and I didn't have any money—I'd had to go quite a bit into debt in tidying up my life, and although I've got quite a good job now I've still got to pay for the furniture in my apartment, and a few other things. So I thought, why the hell not? I get a free trip to Nueva, and it's a place people actually pay a lot of money to go to on vacation. So I wrote back and said I'd go.

"The day before my flight the phone rang in my apartment. I answered it, and a voice said, 'Mrs Caval? I hope you have a good time in Nueva, but watch out for earthquakes.' I said, 'Who is it?' but he rang off without saying anything more. I think it was Charles, but I can't be quite sure, because whoever it was either had or pretended to have a bit of a cold, and spoke in a rather nasal sort of voice.

"I was more angry than worried—it was just the sort of vicious thing that Charles would do, to get me upset and maybe call off the trip. I'd quite got to looking forward to it by then, and all the call did was to make me more than ever determined to go. I'd almost forgotten about it until this morning."

She stopped to drink some coffee. She wasn't looking at me—she was gazing into the night, looking into the distance of her own life, perhaps.

"It's hard to see how it can be anything but an extraordinary coincidence," I said.

"I suppose so." She seemed to speak without much conviction.

"I'm not exactly scared, but I don't know what to do. Edward Caval wants me to go back. I don't think I want to go. But I've spent an awful lot of his money. I didn't owe him anything before, but I feel I do, now."

"I should forget about the money—after all, you lost your things in his house, and naturally he'd want to replace them. And while I don't know anything about his finances, from the look of things he must be pretty rich. How did you get on with him before?"

"Would it sound silly if I said I don't really know? He was wonderfully considerate—treated me like a long-lost grand-daughter, who'd come home. Talked a lot about the past, about how one ancestor had done this, and another that. The nicest thing about him is that he is always so gentle. That made me feel good—after living through the past few years I sort of needed to have a gentle vacation. What I don't know is what, if anything, he got out of me. Once or twice he seemed on the edge of saying something that might explain why he'd invited me, but he never did."

"Were you bored?"

"Not a bit. I'm used to being on my own, and I'd brought some maths books that I'd wanted a chance to study. Living at Chacarima was like being a princess in a children's story—lovely food, everything I wanted, and no one to bother me if I wanted to be alone."

"Why don't you want to go back? Is your vacation nearly up?"

"Lord, no, the university term doesn't start for a couple of months yet. It's just that I feel as if the whole situation had somehow turned unhealthy."

"I don't see why. There's not likely to be another earthquake, and anyway, the house he's gone to is supposed to be away from that particular earthquake belt. Did Mr Caval say that he'd asked me to come back with you?"

"No, he didn't. Are you going, Peter?"

"Would it make any difference?"

She considered this, as if confronted with a problem in maths. "I think perhaps it would," she said. "Unless I started getting frightened of you."

I laughed. "Am I a frightening person?"

"No, but I think maybe you could be."

"I'd better tell you about my own marriage."

"Your marriage? You said you hadn't got a wife."

"I haven't. I had once. It was a long time ago."

The tension that I had felt between us was defused. She laughed—more like a woman who has enjoyed being taken out to dinner.

"So I was right! She couldn't take the sailmaker's kit!"

"She never even saw it. No, it wasn't a bit like that." I gave her a brief account of my leaving the Army, of my years as an industrial tycoon, and of how my marriage and my job had gone together when the firm was taken over. "She needed someone who could afford to keep her—she married my successor in my job," I explained.

"Do you miss her?"

"Not really. I miss the things that marriage might have brought, a proper home, a family ... but marriage with Sybil couldn't have worked out like that. Fortunately I was able to go back to the Army."

"Poor Peter. It seems we've both been rather battered."

I took Ruth back to the hotel, and we arranged to meet for the Nuevan breakfast at eleven-thirty and to leave for Naurataka in the afternoon, in time to get there before dark. She said that she had still a bit of shopping to do, and wanted particularly to see if Fort James could provide her with a few more books. I felt that I ought to call on the brigadier, and, if possible, on the Prime Minister, to let them know my movements.

I found it hard to get to sleep. What an extraordinary story Ruth had told me. There were many things, I was sure, that she had not told me—but then there was really no reason why she should have told me anything at all. Could her story relate in any way to the problem that had brought me to Nueva? It didn't seem likely. But why had Edward Caval wanted her to come from New York? She was not even a relation, merely a remote connection by a now no-longer-existing marriage. What on earth could he want to talk to her about—and if he wanted to talk to her about anything, why hadn't he done so? And why had he never mentioned her ex-husband, who was at least a kinsman? Or was this one of the things on which Ruth had been less than wholly honest?

With these unanswered questions on my mind I could doze only fitfully, and at five-thirty a.m. I was glad to get up. This

39

was not an ungodly time for getting up in Nueva, and I reckoned that if I called on the brigadier around six there would be a good chance of finding him at home.

He was at home, drinking coffee and eating a pineapple on the verandah of his house. He invited me to share both. I began by thanking him for rallying round so promptly yesterday. "We are both soldiers. It was the least I could do," he said.

He asked what were my immediate plans. "I've a fair bit of leave due to me, and having come to Nueva it seems a pity not to take the chance of staying on," I said. "Mr Edward Caval has invited me to stay at a house he has at Naurataka—to make up, perhaps, for his house at Chacarima falling on top of me. I thought I'd accept his invitation, for a few days at any rate."

"Naurataka—that really is the back of beyond! It is very beautiful, though. You can get up into the mountains from there, and if you go you must take the opportunity of visiting one of the Carib settlements. But you will have to go by mule, I think."

"I've travelled by mule-back in my time. I'm ashamed of my ignorance of this part of the world. I know that there are some Carib settlements on the mainland, in the interior of Guyana and Venezuela, but I didn't know that there were any left in the islands."

"There are not many. Those in Dominica are, perhaps, the best known, but there are a few still in Nueva." He paused. "The rest of us, black, white, brown and yellow are all immigrants—the Caribs are our true natives. History has not treated them kindly—or, if death be a preferable alternative to slavery, maybe they were lucky. The Caribs had—indeed, have— a culture of their own, but it could not be adapted to the coming of the Spaniards and other Europeans. They were not prepared to work as slaves on plantations. They fought where they could —bows and arrows against gunpowder, and inevitably they went down. But it was more than that—they simply could not take the life that the Europeans brought, and they just died. You are right in thinking that they almost died out in the islands. There are only a few settlements left."

"How do they live?"

"They live as they have always lived, wonderfully adapted to life in the forest, understanding its resources, and living *with* it rather than just in it. Our Government is sympathetic to them, we have programmes for health and education in the settlements, but I am not sure that they are not happiest when they are left alone. You will meet some of them, I expect."

"I shall certainly try. I also came to talk to you about that lecture you asked me to give."

"It is good of you to remember. Of course I hope you'll be able to give it. I didn't want to remind you about it when you spoke of being on leave."

"Well, that's just a private matter. I came here to do a job, and I'm at your disposal for anything you want me to do."

He seemed pleased at this. "As far as the rifle is concerned, I don't think there is much more to be done," he said. "It speaks —or rather shoots—for itself, particularly when handled as you handled it. I have never seen such shooting. My mind is certainly made up—I want it for our Army. I don't think there will be any difficulty—I'm sure the Government thinks as I do. Having got you here, though, I'd like you to lecture to our Staff course. I'm in charge of Staff training, and you will understand that our resources tend to be limited."

"I shall be glad to do whatever I can. Give me a week, say, at Naurataka, and then if you will fix a date, I'll keep whatever date you suggest."

"Splendid. Will you stay with me when you come back to Fort James?"

"I'd be honoured."

So that was fixed up.

Eight o'clock in the morning seemed an unorthodox hour for calling on Prime Ministers, but Old Government House showed signs of life, and the girl secretary whom I remembered said she thought the Prime Minister was available, and would see me.

Mr Li Cook was as affable and informal as before. "I am thankful that you came to no harm in that unpleasant incident," he said. "And I'm delighted to see that you are taking to our sensible Nuevan hours. The morning for work, the evening for serious conversation, the afternoon for sleep, or perhaps in the right circumstances for love-making." He laughed. "Shall we walk again under the trees?"

His caution seemed grotesque, but it was his business. When we were safely in the shade of *las madres de cacao*, he asked, "How did you get on with Mr Caval?"

"I had scarcely time to get on with him. He gave me a drink,

and we were about to have lunch—sorry, I mean breakfast—
when the house fell on us. For behaviour after an earthquake I
give him high marks—he was calm, cool, and astonishingly
courteous throughout."

"He would be that. Did he strike you as at all a dangerous
man?"

"Dangerous in what context?"

"In wishing to hurt Nueva."

"I shouldn't have said so, but most of the time I spent with
him we were extracting ourselves from the ruins of his house,
and getting across the river to safety. However, he telephoned
last night and invited me to stay with him at another house he
has, at a place called Naurataka. I accepted the invitation, and
I've arranged to go out this afternoon."

"Good. I can rely on your discretion, but it is most important
that I should know what he sees as the future of his estates. . . .
Your other business seems to have turned out well."

"You mean the rifle?"

"Yes. From what Brigadier Ezra tells me you are already
something of a legend as a marksman, and will go down in
Nuevan history."

"It was pure luck."

"Perhaps. Do you know what Napoleon used to ask his
officers when he was considering them for promotion? He did
not ask, 'Are you a good strategist? Can you make good use of
artillery?' but simply, 'Are you a lucky man?' "

"I wonder how they answered!"

"Ah, that is another matter. Perhaps that is why he asked. But
seriously, Colonel, I do not think that your performance with the
Army was just luck. It was the right action at the right time—
though that may be a definition of what men call luck. You did
very well, and I hope you will be as successful in your other
mission."

"I've told the brigadier that I've got some leave due to me,
and that having come to Nueva I'd like to stay on for a bit, and
see something of the island. That leaves me a free hand for the
moment."

"Couldn't be better. When we go back to the office I'll give
you my private telephone number. It is always manned, and a
message there will reach me certainly and quickly."

*　　*　　*

More than half of me did not much like the idea of spying on a man who had invited me to be his guest. But the remaining part of me felt that I could do no harm and might, just possibly, do some good. From the Nuevan point of view the future of the Caval lands on the Atlantic coast was clearly a fairly vital matter, and—although I had not discussed this with the Prime Minister —I was very conscious of the strategic value of the deep-water Chacarima inlet. I was also a little concerned for Ruth. Her part in the Caval story was an enigma, but it was possible that she might need some protection. Whether or not she herself felt this I did not know, but she had seemed a bit relieved that I was going to Naurataka with her.

I got back to the hotel before Ruth, and used the time to call on the manager and arrange for a car to take us out to Mr Caval. I was having a drink on the verandah when Ruth turned up, looking, I thought, remarkably attractive in a plain white linen skirt and a sleeveless cotton blouse. She was carrying a large parcel of books.

"Successful shopping?" I asked.

"Not very. There's a new book on Descartes that I want, but the Neuvan market for Descartes appears to be limited. I could order it from New York, but I'll probably be back before it would get here. But the bookshop is not all that bad, and I got enough to keep me going. What do you read?"

"I travel light. I have a paperback Horace, Helen Waddell's *Medieval Latin Lyrics*, and a translation of Xenophon, also in paperback. I had Latin well beaten into me at school, but I don't know much Greek. At home I find Gibbon adequate for a lifetime's bedside reading, but in seven volumes he's too heavy to carry around."

"Didn't you ever do any maths?"

"I didn't do anything very much. I'm a soldier—I went to Sandhurst at eighteen."

"Well, at least you seem fairly literate for a soldier."

"Don't be impertinent. Sit down and have a drink, and then we'll have lunch—I mean, breakfast. I've ordered a car for this afternoon."

The journey to Naurataka took nearly twice as long as the trip to Chacarima. It wasn't that the distance was all that much farther—it was only about twenty miles more—but the road was a great deal worse. We did not go via Chacarima, because once beyond the Chacarima inlet there is no road along the coast at all. We went more or less through the middle of the island, on a road that climbed and descended in hairpin bends, and for long stretches was distinctly rough. It was breathtakingly beautiful.

Naurataka is directly on the coast. Unlike the Caval "Great House" at Chacarima, which stood alone in miles of parkland, Naurataka House was quite near Naurataka village. It was a fishing village, ending in a small bay, and a breakwater enclosed one shore of the bay, making a harbour where there were several boats. Naurataka House stood on a bluff above the harbour, looking out over the Atlantic. It was quite a climb to get up to it, but once there the view was reward for anything. As we went up by car we scarcely deserved the view.

The butler, Adam, met us as if nothing had ever happened to disturb the civilised Caval life. The house was smaller than Chacarima, but still of considerable size, and the furniture was superb. After we had been shown to our rooms and had a wash, we were conducted to Mr Caval, who was sitting in the usual verandah, with the usual tray of drinks beside him.

He greeted us with all his old courtesy. "It is good of you to return," he said, "and while I naturally regret the unhappy incident at Chacarima I am glad that it has made us come here. In the old days this was the dower house, though my grandmother was the last Caval dowager to live here. I have always kept it up, and try to come here two or three times a year. In some ways I like it better than Chacarima, which always seemed to me a bit ostentatious. But it was convenient for the estate office, and the mill. And the Cavals have always lived at Chacarima. How tied we are to history! Now? Well, I shall certainly not rebuild a Great House at Chacarima, but it may be necessary to have a house of some sort there. For the moment, I am content to be here."

He took his loss, I thought, extraordinarily lightly. "I saw Chacarima House only briefly, but it must have been a priceless possession," I said. "Any expression of sympathy seems quite inadequate. You are meeting your loss, if I may say so, with great courage."

"Courage? I don't think so. There were many beautiful things at Chacarima and I am sad to see them go, but my chief feeling

44

is of thankfulness that no lives were lost. Family documents, and the greater part of our Caval plate, were not at Chacarima. Why have so many old West Indian families slipped out of history? Because of white ants, as much as anything—the ants are relentless destroyers. We had already lost much when I succeeded to the estate, and I was determined to preserve what I could. So I deposited all papers, much plate and other heirlooms, with my old college at Oxford—there is an Oxford connection, because the first Edward Caval to come to Nueva had been an Oxfordshire squire. The college is glad to have them—they use the plate sometimes—and as I was also able to provide an endowment to go with them, everybody has benefited."

He seemed wholly detached. It was getting on for seven o'clock, and the swift tropical nightfall that comes down like a knife was shrouding the Atlantic. The butler came with two oil lamps—there is no electricity at Naurataka—but Mr Caval waved him away. "A few moments yet, Adam, please," he said. And to us, "Do you mind sitting in the twilight? There will be light enough to drink by for ten minutes yet, and I have always loved this hour at Naurataka. It is not day and it is not night, but it holds something of the beauty of both, with an added peace of its own. Soon we shall need the lamps, but not quite yet."

"Do you regret the changes that have come to Nueva?" I asked.

"There has been little change at Naurataka ... but I know what you mean. Regret, I think, is always pointless. I and my family have had much from Nueva. I like to think that we have given a little in return, but our paternal feeling for our people is out of fashion in the politics of today. I suppose many a provincial Roman felt bitterly about the collapse of the Roman Empire—and with reason, for the provinces were swept by barbarism. I cannot say that I feel any particular bitterness about the winding up of the British Empire. It had become, I suppose, an anachronism, although I am less sure that the régimes that have replaced it make for any real improvement in the human lot. But I speak from an exceptionally privileged position, and I wish independent Nueva well." He paused reflectively, then, in a sharper voice, he said, "Look out to sea!"

It was now quite dark on land, and although the sea aways seems to retain some light when it is gone from the land, it was almost dark to seaward. Because we had no lights on the verandah, a speck of light some miles out to sea was clearly visible.

"There is no lighthouse, is there?" I asked. "It must be a ship."

"It is certainly a ship, but what is she doing?"

This seemed a fairly ridiculous question. Why shouldn't there be a ship making her way along the Atlantic coast of Nueva? "Not having a chart, I can't say what her probable passage is," I said. "But shipping must be fairly common in these coastal waters."

"Not nowadays. In the old days, yes, everything went by sea —the West Indian schooner was the lifeblood of the islands, and before there were roads and motor lorries most travel from place to place in Nueva was by schooner. It is still the best way of getting from Naurataka to Fort James—you will recall the road you came by today. The fishermen here take their catch to Fort James in their boats. But the Nauratakans have always been reluctant to sail at night—if they can't get home by nightfall they put into some beach and anchor until daylight. It looks to me as if that vessel is making for the Chacarima Inlet. Why?" He seemed strangely excited.

I didn't know what to say. "Is there a port of any sort there?" I asked.

"No. And no fisherman would go there willingly. You have heard of the Chacarima caves—our local people firmly believe that they are haunted. Even in the old days, when we sent away our sugar by sea, we did not use the inlet, though it offers a magnificent anchorage. Because our people were reluctant to go near the caves, we had to build a jetty on a more exposed beach about five miles to the north."

"Couldn't the ship be making for your jetty?"

"No. You do not know the coast, but if she were, we couldn't see her. Beyond the Chacarima Inlet the coast trends northwards to a promontory, and our jetty is the other side of the promontory."

"Perhaps she is just passing the Nuevan coast, on her way to some other island."

"If so, we shall see the light move along the coast. It looks to me as if it is closing the shore."

It certainly seemed so. Whoever she was, the ship was a long way off, and but for our height above sea-level, we could not have seen her at all. She was far too distant to make out anything but the speck of her lights, and I thought that Caval's eyesight was remarkably good for his age. We continued to watch the light for another ten minutes or so, and then it disappeared. It had not continued along the coast, and therefore, presumably, had put in somewhere. It didn't seem to have anything to do with us.

THE CHACARIMA CAVES

M Y NEXT SURPRISE came with my coffee in the morning. On the tray with coffee and a freshly picked pineapple was an envelope addressed to me, and containing a note from Mr Caval. It said, "Can you please come to my room between six and seven? I shall be most grateful for your advice."

It was then five-thirty. I wasn't yet wholly accustomed to Nuevan hours, but to be served with coffee and delectable fruit around dawn was a splendid way of beginning the day. There was a bathroom next door to my bedroom, and having drunk my coffee in pyjamas I had a shower, and then dressed. I wasn't sure where Caval's room was, but I ought to have known that anything to do with him would be well organised. It was still a little before six, and I thought I'd have a stroll in the grounds of Naurataka House before going to look for him. I explored a grove of orange trees for about ten minutes, and then walked back to the house. Adam, the butler, was at the door to meet me. "Good morning, sir," he said. "Mr Caval is expecting you. Would it be convenient for you to see him?"

Mr Caval's room was really a wing of the house. The butler did not take me to his bedroom but to his sitting-room, a big room with windows along the whole of one side, looking on to the sea. The windows were all open, and I could smell the sea as well as look at it. Caval was standing at one of the windows, and I joined him there. "The nearest land would, I suppose, be Africa," I said.

"Actually, one of the Cape Verde islands, but if you mean mainland it would be somewhere on the coast of Senegal. Three thousand miles of sea—there are few fairer places on the earth's surface." He smiled, but a little absently, I thought.

There was more coffee on a table. He poured a cup for me, and another for himself. "But I did not ask you here to look at the view, lovely as it is," he said. "My son was at Oxford with Sir Edmund Pusey."

"Your son?" I suppose I sounded slightly taken aback, for he went on, "Yes. Doubtless you were told that I have no heir. My son joined the Army in 1939. He was killed at Alamein. It was a long time ago."

I said nothing—there were no words that could have any meaning. There are times when human sympathy can be expressed only by physical contact. This was one of them. Instinctively I held out my hand. He took it, and held it for a moment. Then, "Thank you," he said.

That wretched moment over, he became businesslike again. "As I told you, my son was at Oxford with Edmund Pusey. They were quite close friends, and Pusey spent one Long Vacation with us here. He wrote, of course, when my boy was killed, and we met when I was in England some years ago—when I was fixing up the custody of our family things at Oxford. We exchange letters at Christmas, not much else. However, I had an unexpected letter from him the other day. Here it is." He handed me an envelope, with a note inside in Pusey's handwriting. It said,

Dear Mr Caval,
My old friend Colonel Peter Blair is visiting Nueva for certain negotiations with the Nuevan Government. If you have time, it might interest you to meet him. He is a nice person, and completely reliable.
Yours ever,
Edmund Pusey

How typical of Pusey, I thought. On the face of it, the note meant nothing but a brief social introduction. But "completely reliable" was an odd phrase in such a letter. Casually read, it might not even be noticed, or, if anyone bothered about its meaning, it could be taken as implying no more than Pusey's confidence that I would be socially acceptable. But Sir Edmund was never casual. How much did Caval know about him?

"How interesting," I said lamely.

"If the Prime Minister hadn't got in touch with me about you, I should have been in touch with you directly. As it was, I had no need to. Now I want to ask your advice. Do you think that the incident at Chacarima could have been caused by a bomb of some kind, and not an earthquake?"

It was an extraordinary question. I thought for a moment or

49

two before replying. Then I said, "I have no previous experience of earthquakes—I have a little experience of bombs. It certainly seemed to me like what I imagine to be an earthquake—there was an appreciable period of shaking before the house fell. It was not like the instant explosion of a bomb, and I can recall no sound of an explosion, though in the circumstances it is difficult to be sure. The fire could presumably have been caused by an explosion, though such fires are surely almost inevitable when wooden buildings collapse. Why do you ask?"

"You may think me a little mad, but I assure you I am not. There is a Carib settlement in the mountains a few miles from here, and they grow the best pineapples in Nueva—for generations they have supplied us with pineapples. Yesterday morning a Carib brought a donkey-load of pineapples. He had heard of the calamity at Chacarima—don't ask me how news travels in these isolated places, it just does—and he asked Adam the butler what had happened. Adam explained that there had been an earthquake, at which the Carib shook his head and said, 'No, there could not have been an earthquake. There were none of the signs'.

"Adam brought him to me. I am greatly interested in our few remaining Caribs, and have written a book about them. There is no reason why you should know because it is a highly specialised subject, but I have a degree in anthropology and before I took over the estates I made a considerable study of the indigenous peoples of the Orinoco basin, to whom our Caribs are related. They have an immense fund of traditional knowledge, and are so sympathetic to their natural surroundings that much of their tradition is remarkably accurate. Earthquakes and hurricanes have always been among the natural hazards of their lives, and they claim to have means of foretelling them. Of course the rainmaker cannot always bring rain, but often he can foretell rain long before anybody else can, and is naturally credited with the ability to bring it. So with earthquakes and hurricanes—one cannot accept their forecasts as scientifically based in any way, but one cannot wholly ignore them. This Carib assured me that there could have been no earthquake at Chacarima because this was not the right season for earthquakes, and the leaves on the trees had not twinkled—the behaviour of leaves is one of their means of forecasting. What, then, had happened? I asked. He had an explanation—the Carima river, he said, is angry because of something that is happening in the caves, and it sent a messenger to pull down the house. I asked what was happening in the caves, and he said he did not know. His people do not go there, and with the river in an angry mood they are more than ever determined to keep away. He concluded rather touchingly, 'But it is good for us, because you will now come to live at Naurataka. The river wanted to show its displeasure, but it did not want to hurt you'."

"It was considerate, anyway," I said. "If I may say so, it seems a moving Carib tribute to you."

"We have always been on good terms—indeed, my family has always done what it can to look after the Caribs. They were never enslaved, and in a way that, unhappily, was far from typical of seventeenth- and eighteenth-century planters, we always respected Carib property rights."

"Do you attach any importance to the Carib theory of the earthquake?"

"You mean rationally? It is hard to say. In a sense it is a matter of words: what does cause an earthquake? The underground water-system of the Chacarima caves has never been fully investigated, and is certainly not understood. I suppose it is possible for some surge of water underground to bring about an earth-tremor. I can't see that it matters much. What does matter are the puzzling features of our earthquake—why was it felt over so limited an area? And why, when a house has survived earth-tremors for over a century, should this particular tremor destroy the house and affect nothing else? A bomb would be much more readily explicable."

"That would imply that someone wants to bomb you. Have you any reason to suppose that there is such a someone?"

He was silent for what seemed a long time. Then he said, "Colonel Blair, I must accept the credentials that Sir Edmund Pusey gives you. I have no one else in whom I can confide, and, as I have said, I need advice. . . . The Prime Minister will have given you an outline of Caval history, I suppose?"

I nodded, and he went on, "It is in all the guide-books, anyway—it is a romantic story. And it is true that the two branches of the Caval family have never been on good terms, a hostility made worse by the fact that the Edward Cavals have kept their lands and maintained a flourishing business, whereas the Antoine Cavals have mostly been heavily in debt. I have no wish to slander Nicolas and Charles, the present representatives of the

Antoine Cavals, but I know no good of either. Nicolas is shrewd, and sees opportunities for himself in island politics, Charles, his son, has brains, but he does not seem to be in any way an estimable character. I have made it my business to find out about him, and I do not like what I have found.

"The death of my only son may seem to offer some hope of ultimate triumph for the Antoine Cavals, for with my death my line dies out. Could it be of any advantage to them to hasten my death? I have asked myself this question, and I cannot answer it, because I do not know what calculations they may make. I am by far the largest landowner in Nueva, and much of the capital, Fort James, belongs to me, as do many of the island's businesses. In slightly different circumstances I should have been extremely vulnerable when Nueva became independent—'Down with the big landlord' is nearly always a popular cry. But the Nuevan people have never been hostile to me—indeed, they have never shown me anything but kindness and respect. My businesses are all, in a sense, co-operatives: I take little out of them, and those who work for me on the whole do well. We have not got a revolutionary Government—for what it's worth, enjoyment of the rights of private property is written into our constitution. Of course times change: the day of great estates is no doubt over, and I do not know for how long the Caval estates can remain intact. As things are, there is no indication of any powerful wish to overthrow me.

"Apart, that is, from the Nicolas Cavals. My death would certainly create a new situation on the island. Should I die intestate, it is possible that Nicolas could establish a claim to be my heir. It is even possible that he could attempt to challenge my will, on the ground that the original grant from Charles II established a sort of entail of the property to the heirs of the body of the Edward Caval to whom the grant was made. He would not succeed. The terms of the grant were the basis of the law-suit by which the second Edward Caval tried to dispossess Antoine from the share of the island left to him by will, and the English courts ultimately found against him. Such a case now would be in the Nuevan court, but we have inherited English law, and I cannot see a Nuevan court upholding the narrowest interpretation of a royal grant made over 300 years ago, an interpretation, moreover, already rejected by much more nearly contemporary English courts. Still, he might think it worth a try.

"There is another possible calculation. I am naturally proud of the Caval name, and sad that after three centuries there should be no Caval of my own line to follow me. Nicolas and Charles may calculate that whatever my feelings about them personally I shall leave the estates to one of them rather than break the Caval connection. I may say that this was once my own thought, and it was for this reason that I had such detailed inquiries made about Charles. From what I have learned, in no circumstances would I now leave him a cent."

"You have talked about the Caval family. Are there, perhaps, political motives that might prompt an attack on you? I am not at all informed about Nuevan politics, but you cannot be in Nueva long without learning that there is some dispute about the direction that development should take. I have heard that one school of thought would like to see large-scale development of this coast for tourism, but that others hold that the tourist industry, though it can be profitable in the short run, is liable to blight the island's future. Since it is all your land, is it possible that the pro-tourist party might want you out of the way?"

"It is possible, I suppose. The Prime Minister is, on the whole, against excessive development of tourism—as he puts it, 'We do not want Nueva to become a brothel for millionaires.' I'm sure he's right, but the temptations are real, and the Opposition wants to attract more American money. But the argument is really fairly marginal. No one suggests that there should be no tourists in Nueva. We have a vigorous Tourist Board, and in the past few years we have built a number of new hotels. I should hate to see the whole of this coast subject to the kind of development that had corroded so many other places, but I am no stick in the mud. I have leased several bays nearer to Fort James for the building of hotel complexes, and have put up some of the capital for them. I do not campaign against tourists—I take no active part in politics. The Government knows that I should not be a willing seller of more land for tourism, but my feelings are not really of much importance. A different Government could acquire my land by compulsory purchase—there is not much that I could do about it. I do not see that my death would have much bearing on the matter one way or another."

"May I ask you a question? Why did you invite Ruth Caval, Charles Caval's ex-wife, to stay with you?"

"So she told you about Charles? Well, I had a number of

53

reasons, some of which I may explain later, but I should prefer not to go into them now. I have a request to make of you. Would you make a visit to the Chacarima caves? I could go myself, but you have seen how fast news travels, and I do not wish to show any particular interest in the caves. But I do want to know if anything is going on there that I should know about. It would be quite natural for you, and perhaps Ruth, to go as sightseers. I can send Adam with you as a guide. He will not much like it because he is afraid of the caves, but he will certainly go with you. And he knows the parts that visitors go to—indeed, he knows them quite as well as I do, for he and I used to adventure there as boys together. As a boy with me he wasn't much worried, but he grew up to be afraid of the caves as all the local people are. He won't mind them so much if you are with him. I was wondering if you would go today?"

"By all means. How do we get there?"

"You can go by road, but you have almost got to go back to Fort James. By far the easiest way is to go by boat. It is no more than about fifteen miles by sea. I have already arranged for a schooner from the harbour to be available this morning. If you are ready, we might walk down there now. If you leave by eight you should be at the caves well before midday—the trade wind hardly ever fails."

At the front door we met Ruth, who had also been wandering in the garden. "What a lovely morning!" she said. And to me, "I was wondering where you'd got to. I knocked on your door to ask you to come for a walk, but you weren't there."

"I can ask you to come for a sail. I'm going to visit the Chacarima caves. Would you like to come?"

"Is Mr Caval coming?"

"No," Caval said. "I have a lot of tiresome letters to write. But do go with Colonel Blair. There's a boat ready in the harbour —we're on our way down now."

"I'd love to. Do I need anything?"

"A swimsuit and a towel, perhaps."

"Right, I'll go and get them. What about you, Peter? Are you going to swim?"

"I don't know, but I might as well take my things. I'll come up with you."

We were on board soon after half-past seven.

The *Grand Duchess* had been brought up to the quay. She was about eighty feet long, with the traditional Caribbean schooner-rig. I learned later that she had been island-built, in a bay on the Caribbean coast of Nueva, where a village community of boatbuilders had been established since the seventeenth century—originally (or so it was said) by a ship's carpenter who had deserted from an English merchantman, fathered numerous children by a harem of Negro women, taught them all boat-building, and created a thriving business in ship-repair work for buccaneers, who put in to careen their ships. In time the buccaneers departed, but the tradition of boatbuilding stayed on, and in the heyday of the schooner trade Nuevan-built schooners were considered among the best in the Caribbean. They were built with few tools other than adze and saw, but the finished woodwork was a joy to look at. The original ship's carpenter was reputed to be a Devon man, and there was a slight look of Brixham about the *Grand Duchess*. Adam the butler was on board when we got down to her, and we were introduced to her master, Captain Amos, and his crew of three.

"Does she belong to you?" I asked the skipper.

"No, sir, she is Mr Caval's ship, but he lets us use her for runs to Fort James, and sometimes to the other islands if people want to go there."

We cast off almost at once. Mr Caval waved from the quay, and we were away.

The trade wind that brought Columbus to the West Indies is a magnificent wind, blowing still as it has since our globe began spinning. Its regularity and reliability are enshrined on the map in the Caribbean archipelagoes called the Windward and the Leeward Islands. If ever an area of the earth's surface was made for the sailing boat the West Indies are, and it is an example of man's catastrophic waste of his resources that the thousands of millions of free horsepower provided by the wind are now largely unused. Nueva seemed to me to be just about ideally placed to benefit from the trade wind. It counts, I suppose, among the Windward Islands, but lying south of Dominica and north of Martinique it is on the edge of the group, with a good reaching wind, the best point of sailing for a schooner, available practically all the time. I liked the way Captain Amos and his crew got off from the quay. The *Grand Duchess* had a staysail rig, and she got away under a big staysail set from her foremast, and a smallish jib. When we were safely out her big mainsail went up, and an inner, larger jib. It was a soldier's wind, and she soon began to tramp along the coast. I reckoned that she was probably doing around six or seven knots.

It was sheer joy to be at sea again, and the white of the wave-tops against the marvellously blue sea and the green of the forested coast made an unforgettable picture. I wasn't allowed to enjoy it at once, for Adam the butler appeared in the companionway and told us that coffee was served. I couldn't disappoint him, so Ruth and I went below. The saloon was a mariner's joy. It was simply, even sparsely, furnished, with a cabin table and a pair of long settee berths, but the woodwork was all purple-heart, a superb local hardwood, polished to a mirror-finish. We were offered coffee and bananas picked that morning. I dutifully drank a cup and ate a banana, and then said that I'd like to go on deck again.

Captain Amos was at the wheel, and I asked if I could take her for a bit. He was dubious: there was a fair weight of wind, and he didn't want his sails tied up in knots by a landlubber helmsman. I explained that I had spent much of my life at sea in sailing boats, and that I wouldn't let the schooner get into any trouble. He then handed over the wheel, but watched me warily. I thought that she'd be happier if the sheets were hardened a little, and suggested this. He smiled, and nodded. "But it may not be quite so comfortable—she will heel more," he said. But I wanted to get the feel of the schooner at her best, so I asked him to carry on. He nodded again, called one of the crew, and hardened the sheets. She felt the improvement at once, threw up a fine bow-wave with her forefoot, and probably put on about half a knot. After about ten minutes the skipper apparently felt that he could have confidence in me, and went below to have a cup of coffee himself.

I kept an eye on a small house-flag, presumably the Caval house-flag, that she was wearing, but it stayed stiff as a board. This wonderful wind was not in the least fluky, and I relaxed in the simple delight of handling her. She was as responsive as a yacht, and the wheel had that lovely sense of being alive under my fingers. As the *Grand Duchess* and I came to terms with

56

each other, and I realised that she knew very well how to look after herself, my thoughts went back to my·strange conversation with Caval. What a bewildering hotch-potch of conflicting predictions about earthquakes! There was Ruth's extraordinary statement about the prediction in New York, and then the equally extraordinary piece of Carib folklore or witch-doctoring which insisted that there hadn't been an earthquake at all. Ruth, I had felt at the time and felt more strongly now, had almost certainly lied, or at least had tried deliberately to cloud the truth. I was sure that she knew who it was who telephoned her, and that it was not her ex-husband. Why did she want to be secretive? And what could it matter in talking to me, a chance acquaintance wholly detached from her own affairs? And why on earth had Caval· sought her out and invited her to come to Nueva? His interest in Charles was understandable: obviously he had considered making Charles his heir, and presumably he had employed some high-grade American agency to have inquiries made about him. From what he had learned, Charles was out. Then why go out of his way to establish some kind of relationship with Charles's ex-wife? And if Caval really wanted my advice, why not be frank with me so that I had the facts on which I could advise?

And what was the Pusey relationship? It was typical of Sir Edmund that he should send me to Nueva knowing nothing of Edward Caval, and leave me to find out about him for myself. Why, then, write to Caval about me? And did Caval know anything about Pusey's real job? And why was the Prime Minister so anxious that I should do his dirty work for him, and find out things that, as I saw it, he could readily have discovered for himself? Before I knew Caval I could imagine reasons why the head of the Nuevan Government might not wish to be directly involved in any dealings with him that had obvious political implications. But Caval wasn't like that. He was naturally a little sad that his feudal empire was on its way out, but he had no hostility to Nuevan independence, and as far as I could assess things wanted nothing but the long-term good of Nueva. None of it made sense.

If I could get nowhere with my thinking, the *Grand Duchess* was making remarkably good progress with our voyage. She must certainly have been doing seven knots, for it was barely two hours after our departure from Naurataka when Captain Amos pointed to the headland that marked the entrance to the Chacarima Inlet.

57

"We have about two miles to go," he said, "and I think I'd better take her now, for I know the entrance. It is not difficult, but the Carima river sometimes runs strongly, and there are some tricky currents where it meets the sea."

Ruth had gone forrard and was holding on to one of the foremast shrouds, watching the coast as we stood in. I joined her, and we stood together as we rounded the headland and opened the entrance to the inlet. The *Grand Duchess* came off the wind as she turned to go in, and the skipper ordered the staysail handed, and the bigger of her two jibs. He let out the remaining sheets, and she ran sweetly into the inlet. It was about half a mile wide, and we had about a mile to go to reach the anchorage for the caves. We anchored in about five fathoms off a beach of brilliant white sand. It was just on ten o'clock.

Adam the butler came up to us. "Breakfast will be ready in an hour, sir," he said. "There is not time to go to the caves before breakfast. Would you and madam like to take a swim now, and go ashore after breakfast? It is safe to swim here. Sharks hardly ever come into the inlet, but we shall have a lookout, of course."

"I'd love to go in," Ruth said. "I've never seen water of such a brilliant colour—it will be like swimming in the sky."

Through the saloon, the *Grand Duchess* had four small cabins, two to starboard, two to port. One was allotted to me and one to Ruth. We changed quickly and went back on deck. Some boarding steps had been lowered to make it easy for us to get to the water, but Ruth dived in straight from the deck. She dived beautifully, and swam like a fish. Her dark hair gleaming in the sunlight on blue water, she waved to me. I am not all that brilliant as a diver, but I couldn't go in from a ladder when she had dived from the deck. So I followed her, mercifully without making too ungainly a splash. "I'll race you to the beach," I said. She was a much more graceful swimmer than I, but she hadn't my strength, and I'm glad to say that I won, though not by much. Honour satisfied, we walked a little way up the beach and found a rock to sit on.

"This is what I call a real vacation," she said.

"You're a beautiful swimmer."

"Well, when I was a kid my parents had a little summer house on Martha's Vineyard, and I used to spend most of our time there in the water. I didn't know you could handle a schooner."

"I told you that I was brought up in small boats."

"I don't call the *Grand Duchess* small. I thought you did very well."

"I thought you stayed below eating bananas."

"Well, I kept an eye on you. I thought, perhaps, I'd have to take to swimming earlier."

"We'd better get back to the lunch they call breakfast—if you haven't eaten too many bananas to spoil your appetite."

The beach to which Ruth and I had swum was enclosed in a small bay on the northern shore of the Chacarima Inlet. The western end of the bay was a steep cliff, and beyond the cliff was the sea-entrance to the caves. The anchorage off the beach was about a quarter of a mile from the caves. We went in the *Grand Duchess*'s dinghy, a tough twelve-foot boat, clinker-built, and equipped with an outboard engine. Only Adam, Ruth and I went —Captain Amos and his crew obviously had no wish to go near the place. We were provided with a lantern torch apiece, and two big acetylene lamps. We also took a coil of line.

The outboard was well maintained, and fired at once. The trip round the cliff to the entrance took only a few minutes. I kept my eyes open for any sign of other people, but there was none. If the mysterious light of last night had been a vessel making for the Chacarima Inlet, she was gone.

I was astonished by the sheer size of the entrance—it was the most enormous archway I had ever seen. What from the little beach had seemed to be a cliff was the scarp of a hillside, or rather range of hills, thickly wooded, and climbing to at least 3,000 feet. The hills fell steeply to the sea—beyond our little beach there were no more beaches, but steep-to, perpendicular cliffs. Penetrating into these cliffs was an arm of the sea, entering through an arch at least 200 yards wide, and certainly several hundred feet high.

"Is this the sea, or the mouth of the Carima river?" I asked Adam.

"It is both, sir," he said. "The river goes underground about three miles away. How it flows through the caves no one knows. Here, at the mouth, the water is still salt, and it is salt for as far inside as I have ever been, so the sea goes in a long way."

Adam was at the tiller. He took us in through the middle of the arch, and then throttled back, so that we went on quite slowly. The arch was so huge that there was light for some distance inside, but it gradually grew dimmer, and when we got to a natural rock-quay that was used as a landing-place, it was like being inside an unlighted cathedral at dusk. As our eyes grew accustomed to the dimness we could see well enough to get ashore. There was an iron ring let into the rock, and Adam tied the boat to this. "It was put in by Mr Caval's father," he said. "He liked to bring visitors to the caves."

The rock at this point was low enough to climb on to, and once up we were on a rock ledge, about ten or a dozen feet wide. Adam lit both the acetylene lamps. He placed one on the rock above the boat, "So that we can see to come back," he said. He took the other himself, and gave torches to Ruth and me. Leading the way with the big acetylene lamp he began to walk along the ledge towards the interior of the cavern.

It was easy going for about a quarter of a mile. The ledge remained wide, and climbed quite gently. We were following the sea—or the river. I shone my torch downwards every now and again, and saw that though we were steadily gaining height above sea-level we were still at the water's edge. Then we came to a jumble of broken rock, blocking the ledge. "It is possible to climb the rocks," Adam said, "and then there is a sort of path continuing into the mountain. But it is a stiff climb, and there is nothing to see. We will go to the right—do you see a sort of doorway between two rocks? There is a good path beyond it, into another part of the caves."

We followed him through this gap in the rocks, Ruth next to him, and I bringing up the rear. The path narrowed, and began to climb more steeply, but it was still quite easy walking. Geologically it was a weird formation—rather like a chimney that you meet in rock-climbs, but obviously not a fault running through the rock because it did not go to the bottom of the cliff but ended in a firm ledge between rock-walls, the ledge on which we were walking. And it did not go to the top, because it was roofed. How high above us the rock roof was I could not make out—I shone my torch upwards, but the beam could not reach wherever the roof might be. I could only assume that we were in a sort of steep tunnel, cut by water in some remote past.

Again we came to a rock-fall, and again we could continue by making a dog-leg turn to the right. Now the path was much narrower—in places barely eighteen inches wide—and much steeper. And we began to hear a noise, a bit like that of an express train in the distance. As we went on the noise got louder, and suddenly our path came to an end, with two iron bars placed across it. The bars guarded a sheer drop of Heaven knows what depth. Adam shone his acetylene lamp downwards, and there, far below, was water. Then he turned the lamp to the left, and Ruth and I simply gasped with wonder. We were looking at a cliff of moving water, where the Carima river plunged over some underground precipice to form a tremendous waterfall. How wide it was I could not tell, for the light could not reach across it. The waterfall formed one side of a gigantic cavern, with the river at the bottom. No roof, no other wall was visible. The river seemed to me to be flowing to the right, that is, away from the sea-entrance to the caves, but presumably it twisted and turned underground to get there. The waterfall, the cavern, and the whole surroundings of the place were so stupendous that I didn't realise for a moment that Adam was speaking. I had to make a deliberate effort of will to bring myself back to listen to him. "These bars are also the work of Mr Caval's father," he said. "Many years ago, when the present Mr Caval and I were boys, there was a tragedy when a visitor to Chacarima fell over. He was never seen again—the river took his body as well as his spirit. So Mr Caval put the bars to protect visitors. He had to do the work himself, helped by Mr Edward and me, for people said that the river would not like it. I do not know if it is so. There are not many visitors. I do not much like coming here, but Mr Caval asked me to take you, and I am glad that you have seen the most wonderful sight in Nueva, perhaps in the whole world. There is no more to see. If you are ready, let us now return to the boat."

I should have liked to go down into the cavern, but it would have required ropes and climbing equipment, and better lighting than we had. Also, it was clear that Adam was on tenterhooks to get away. So we reversed ourselves for Adam to lead the way down, I again bringing up the rear, about half a dozen yards behind Ruth.

When we got to the first dog-leg turn—that is, the second turn of our ascent—I stopped for a moment to examine the rock-fall that blocked the chimney leading away from the sea-cave. The jumble of rocks seemed quite natural, and I was about to move on when my torch shone on something that looked like a fragment of cloth. It was caught under a boulder. I tried to pick it up, but it wouldn't come away. I looked more closely, and saw that it was the hem of a pair of khaki shorts. Then I realised that there was a leg clothed by the shorts, and the rest of a body under the rubble of stones.

Ruth and Adam hadn't noticed that I'd stopped, and, walking downhill, were forty to fifty yards ahead. I called out to them, my shout echoing eerily in the tomb-like passage. They came back, Ruth running, Adam following her reluctantly.

Ruth's torch, added to the light from mine, showed that the boulder covered all the lower part of a body except for a small area of one leg, just above the knee. Above the boulder was a heap of smaller stones. "Bring the big lamp," I called to Adam.

The powerful acetylene beam illuminated the whole pile of rocks and stones. As soon as he saw the leg Adam screamed, "Don't touch it, Colonel sir. The river is angry. We must go at once."

"We can't go. There's probably nothing we can do, but we can move those small stones from his chest and face. It's just conceivable that he's still alive. We can't leave him until we know."

Adam was trembling so much that the acetylene lamp wavered, and I thought he was going to drop it. I took it from him, and stood it on a rock. Then I put an arm round Adam's shoulders, and helped him to sit down. "Try not to worry, old chap," I said as gently as I could. "The river has no reason to be angry with us—maybe it brought us here to help."

The old man just moaned.

Leaving him sitting on the ground, his back propped against a wall of the passage, I turned to the stones. "Can you hold both torches, Ruth?" I said. "I must see if I can uncover his head."

Ruth was splendid. She didn't need to be asked where to direct the beams, but shone them precisely where I needed them. Estimating from the position of the leg roughly where the head would be, I climbed over the big boulder and lifted away the rubble of smaller stones. I started a bit too low, for I began by uncovering his chin. I soon had the rest of the face uncovered, and then it was apparent that we could indeed do nothing. The man, a white man, was unquestionably dead, and there was a bullet wound in his left temple.

He was lying on his back, so that the light of the torches was full on his face. But only for a moment. Suddenly they wavered as Ruth collapsed. "Oh no, Oh no, Oh no," she said as she passed out.

Scrambling down to go to Ruth, I knocked away a few more stones from the man's chest, uncovering a shirt pocket. In it was a small black notebook. Without really thinking what I was doing I put it in my own pocket.

V

ON THE RUN

I H A D N O water, but I rubbed Ruth's hands, and in a minute or two she sat up. "Sorry, Peter," she said. "What do we do now?"

"The first thing is to see what we can do for Adam. He seems in a bad way."

The old butler wasn't sitting, but rather slumped on the path, and his head had fallen forward. I slipped my hand under his shirt, but could feel no heartbeat. His eyes were closed. Gently I lifted one of his eyelids, but there was no response. "I'm horribly afraid that he's gone, too," I said. "Let's get him lying down properly, and I'll see if I can massage his heart."

I took off my own shirt, folded it to make a pillow, and laid the old man's head on it. Ruth and I then straightened his limbs. He had certainly stopped breathing. Recalling what I could of First Aid courses in the Army I tried giving him the so-called "kiss of life", but he did not respond. Then I tried massaging his chest and rib-cage. We worked away for half an hour, but it was no good: the angry river had claimed another victim.

"I suppose we could get him back to the boat, but without a stretcher it would be an appalling job," I said. "And it would take a long time. The best thing now is for us to go back to try to get help. Also, the body under the stones must be reported as soon as possible."

I put on my shirt again, we laid out the old man as decently as we could, and set off back to the boat. This time I went first, carrying the acetylene lamp and one of the torches. Ruth kept very close behind me. There was no difficulty about finding the way—we had simply to follow the path, and turn through the rock-opening that led to the ledge by the sea. I had a private panic that somehow we might miss this opening, but we didn't—there was no other way to go. All the same it was with a sense of infinite relief that we found ourselves back in the great sea-cave, and saw the light from the other acetylene lamp left by the boat. We ran the rest of the way to it. It was sheer heaven to be in the boat, returning to daylight and the clean sea. The *Grand Duchess*, lying peacefully at anchor, seemed almost too good to be true.

Captain Amos met us at the top of the boarding-ladder. He could see that there was something wrong. Why was Adam not with us? I explained hurriedly, and asked if he and two of the crew would come back with us to recover Adam's body. "We can rig a stretcher out of a piece of sail and two oars," I said.

To my bewilderment—and anger—Captain Amos flatly refused to come. "The river is angry after the earthquake," he said. "It is not good for anybody to go into the caves. Look what has happened to Mr Adam."

There was nothing for it but to accept the situation, but it was a problem to know what best to do. The *Grand Duchess* had no radio. She did, however, have a map, and from the map it seemed that the sugar-mill and offices of the Chacarima Estate were not much more than three miles from the head of the Chacarima Inlet. I asked Captain Amos if he would put me ashore there, and then take Ruth and the schooner back to Naurataka. From the sugar-mill I could at least telephone the authorities at Fort James and report what had happened.

He agreed to this. Ruth wanted to come with me, but it seemed better that she should go back to Mr Caval. Also, although the map showed a track running from the inlet to the sugar-mill, the whole area was thickly forested, and I had no idea what the track was like. Captain Amos let me take the map, and I had the small wrist-compass that I had put on that morning—I wear it as automatically as my watch whenever I go off anywhere.

One of the sailors put me ashore, and took the boat back to the *Grand Duchess*. I did not wait to see her leave, but struck off into the bush.

The main stream of the Carima river apparently ran into the caves, but there was a river, about twenty yards wide, at the head of the inlet. I remembered that we had to cross a river to get from Chacarima House to the sugar-mill, and I made sure of landing on the side of the river that I reckoned the mill to be on. I needed the compass. There was indeed a track of sorts, but it was much overgrown, and met various other trails—possibly drinking-trails by which animals got to the river. The track climbed steeply, but although it was hard going the climb turned out to be a help, for when I got to the ridge I could see the chimney of the sugar-mill, and after that there was no chance of going wrong.

On the walk I wondered what to do. The office manager would know how to get hold of the police, but how quickly they would act I didn't know. I decided to ring the private number that the Prime Minister had given me—murder in what to him was a sensitive area of the island certainly justified the use of it.

The manager remembered me. He showed horror and shock at my story, and at once took me to a telephone. The Nuevan telephone service, at least between Chacarima and Fort James, was better than I expected, and I got through in less than five minutes. What is more, I got through to the Prime Minister himself. He let me speak without asking any questions. Then he said, "This may be exceedingly important. I will send out the Chief of Police, and also, I think, a small detachment of the Army straight away. Can you wait at the Chacarima mill until they get there?"

"Of course," I said.

Feeling that I'd done what I could, I then tried to telephone Caval at Naurataka. But in this I was less successful. After being asked repeatedly to hold on, a telephone voice finally told me that there was trouble on the line, and that it was unlikely that a call could be got through that day. "I am afraid it often happens so," the manager said. "Part of the line runs through the forest, and branches fall on it. Often it is quicker to go by road to Naurataka than to try to telephone." I considered asking him to send a man with a note to Caval, but it seemed pointless— Ruth would get back by sea long before anyone could get there by road.

The road from Fort James to the inhabited district of Chacarima was quite good, and a staff car and two jeeps turned up before I was expecting them. They seemed to be all Army, no police. An immaculate young captain got out of the car. "Colonel Blair?" he asked.

"Yes."

"I have orders to place you under arrest."

I was so astonished that for a moment I could say nothing at all. Then I asked, "What on earth for?"

"That, sir, is not my business. I have simply to carry out my orders. May I have your pistol?" The young captain was very correct.

"I haven't got a pistol."

"Very good, sir. Will you please come with me now?"

"But what about the Chacarima caves? There are two dead men there. Are you just going to leave them?"

"Again, sir, that is not my business. I am instructed to take you in custody to Fort James. Please do not delay."

He had a sergeant and half a dozen soldiers with him. There was nothing I could do. The sergeant opened the door of the car, and I got in. We set off at once, a jeep leading the way, and then the staff car, with the second jeep bringing up the rear. The captain sat beside me in the back seat of the car. He didn't seem inclined for conversation, but sat looking stonily in front of him.

I tried to figure out what could have happened, but the whole proceedings seemed so lunatic that nothing I could think of made any sense at all. The order for my arrest could have come only from the Prime Minister—or had the Army taken over from the Prime Minister? What was I supposed to have done? I had reported the finding of a dead body in the Chacarima caves—was it to be suggested that I had killed him? Adam, the only Nuevan witness to the finding of the body, was dead. Ruth was a witness, but it would take some time to get hold of her, and would she be believed? Would she be regarded as my accomplice? Accomplice in what? Caval seemed to think that somebody wanted him out of the way. It had seemed wildly improbable when he talked about it, but now I wasn't so sure. I ought at least to try to warn him and Ruth. But how could I, when I was myself in custody, and even if I could get to a telephone the line to Naurataka was apparently out of action.

The road from the sugar-mill climbed steadily for the first five miles or so, winding through thickly forested country towards the central ridge of the island. Near the summit of the ridge, the leading jeep stopped. Then we stopped, too—a large branch had fallen across the road. There was plenty of manpower to move it, and the captain got out to see to it. He left his door open. Acting on the spur of the moment I got out too, and ran from the road into the bush.

It took the military party a minute or so to realise what was happening, and that gave me an invaluable start. It was wonderful country for a fugitive, rocky and densely wooded between the outcrops of rock. I began by plunging downhill, but as this was the obvious way to try to escape I doubled round a rocky spur and went uphill again. Soon I was well above the road, and I climbed into a tree. The thick tropical foliage hid me completely, but I could look out to see what was happening. A soldier fired a couple of shots in the vague direction of my jump from the road, but it was obvious that they weren't aimed at anything. It also seemed that nobody had any thought that I might have doubled back uphill. The captain sent men rushing in all directions downhill, but no search party came above the road. The course of wisdom seemed to be to stay where I was.

They searched for an hour, and then the captain had a short conference with the sergeant, with much pointing downhill, and back the way we had come. I could see what was happening, but was too far off to hear anything of what was said. Piecing together what I could from gestures and pointing, I reckoned that they had decided that I would be trying to get back to the mill, where, presumably, I might obtain transport. Anyway, the party returned to the vehicles, and with some trouble, for the road was narrow, turned round and went back the way we'd come. I waited for them to get out of sight and then climbed down from my tree and continued making my way up the ridge.

I had the map that I'd brought ashore from the *Grand Duchess*, and my wrist-compass. I hadn't much confidence in the map—it had been wrong at least twice on the route from the inlet to the mill—but at least it showed the general lie of the northern part of the island. Could I get to Naurataka before anyone thought of looking for me there? As the crow flies, it wasn't much more than eighteen miles—but I wasn't a crow, and the country was wooded and difficult. In a way this helped, for the only road to Naurataka went an immensely long way round, going right over to the other side of the island. And difficult as the country was I could follow a more or less direct route along the ridge, not coming down until I had to make the descent to Naurataka Bay. If I could keep near the summit of the ridge the vegetation would be a trifle thinner.

I couldn't hope to do it, though, before dark. My compass was luminous, so I could follow a compass course all right, but could I cover very rough ground in the dark without falling and breaking something? And how could I know at what point to begin the descent to Naurataka?

From the ridge I could see the sea. I had a superb view of the Chacarima Inlet, and of the wide bay beyond the headland that enclosed the inlet. Naurataka Bay was the next bay along the coast. The moon was about half-full. If the night was clear, and at that time of year it probably would be, I ought to be able to make out the sea, and the land-masses of the headlands. That should be enough to give me rough directions for beginning the descent.

The day seemed to have gone on for ever, but it had started early, and it was still only five o'clock. I could count on another hour or so of light, and half an hour of twilight. The thing was to get going at once, to make the most of the light, and after that I'd have to trust to luck.

It was a hellish walk, but in some ways less hard than I'd feared. The ridge was a true summit, and by keeping as nearly as I could to its crest I was on the watershed, and didn't have to struggle with the ravines that cut up the hillside lower down. And the going could have been much worse. I wasn't actually above the tree-line, but I was above the line of the bigger tropical trees, and, more important, above the line of the fierce growth of lianas and dense bush that filled the lower slopes of the forest. I had no food, which didn't matter much, and no water, which did, for I began to be desperately thirsty. Just before it got dark, however, I heard the sound of running water, and coming down a bit from the ridge of the watershed I found the runnel of a little stream emerging from a group of rocks. It was exquisitely clear and cold. I cupped my hands and drank as much as I could. I wished I could carry some with me, but I had nothing to carry water in. This bothered me, for I had a long night march ahead, and I knew that I should get thirsty again. The tropics, though, are kindly to primitive man—or to modern man reduced to fairly primitive lack of possessions. A few yards below the stream was a clump of vine-like plants, rather like huge vegetable marrows gone mad, which bore a crop of hard-skinned gourds. Mercifully I had my knife—a good seaman's clasp-knife that I have carried for years. I cut one of the gourds, scooped out the pithy inside, and was left with a container that held about two pints of water. From the thick stem of one of the

69

plants I cut a section that served quite well as a cork, and I climbed back to the ridge to continue my journey, feeling much happier.

By the time it was dark I reckoned that I'd covered about five miles. That left thirteen miles or so to go. The next hour was slow going, because the half-moon wasn't up, and my eyes were not acclimatised to the dark. I doubt if I covered much more than a mile, but after that things got better. The moon didn't give much light, but enough to make out the shapes of the larger rocks, and, to my relief, enough to make out the sea and the dark land-masses of the headlands. After two hours I stopped for a quarter of an hour's rest, and drank half my water. Then I carried on, and by one o'clock in the morning I reckoned that I'd rounded—inland—the last headland before Naurataka Bay, and that it was time to descend. The descent was the roughest, and the hardest, part of the trip. I decided to follow a watercourse, which was bound to lead down to the bay, but it soon became a typical steep-sided ravine. The stream flowed at the bottom, with no path—there was water to the edge of the rock-walls of the ravine. But it wasn't deep, and I could walk *in* it, scrambling over rocks as I came to them. I threw away my gourd—I had no more need to carry water, and I did need both hands free. I nearly met disaster when the stream went over an edge of rock to form a waterfall, but I heard and identified the sound about a hundred yards before I got there. The fall was only about ten feet high, but in the darkness it seemed as formidable as the North face of the Eiger. I ended up soaked to the skin but still in one piece, and carried on.

The waterfall was the worst stretch of the whole journey. After the fall the stream widened, and on one bank there was a ledge that became a sort of path. By two o'clock I was on the outskirts of Naurataka village, and it was plain walking to get to Naurataka House.

I didn't know if the Army or the police had got there ahead of me. Thinking that the place might, perhaps, be picketed I went as carefully as I could, moving from tree-shadow to tree-shadow, and waiting for a moment after each move to listen for any sound. But there was nothing, and when I got to the house it seemed sleeping undisturbed.

What to do now? I tried the front door, but it was locked. I didn't want to wake up the place, so I decided to try to climb in. The problem was the verandah. It wasn't an external verandah, with a roof, but built, as in all the older Nuevan houses, as an extension to the ground-floor rooms, so that the roof of the verandah was simply part of the floor of the rooms over it. But there were some wooden pillars making supports for latticed shutters, normally left open. Helped by the slats of one of the shutters I managed to climb a pillar, and reaching up, I could just get my fingers on the edge of a window-sill belonging to one of the bedrooms. There was a small cavity at the top of the pillar where the wood had rotted away. I got a toe in this and, with a heave and a prayer, I was up and on to the window-sill.

As on all tropical nights when it isn't the rainy season the window was open. Whose room was it? It wasn't mine, but it was on the same side of the house, and I took a chance on its being either Ruth's room, or unoccupied. Coming from the outside night into the house I could see nothing at all—the room was pitch-dark. I waited on the window-sill while my eyes adjusted themselves until I could just make out shapes, and then I saw that the big mosquito net which covers all Nuevan beds was down. Presumably, then, there was someone sleeping there. It wasn't the servants' part of the house, and I didn't think it could be Caval, for he had a set of rooms in another wing. Unless some other guest had turned up, it must be Ruth. I went to the edge of the net and pulled it back. There was a shape of dark hair on the white pillow. Yes, it must be Ruth. I put my hand on her shoulder.

She started up with a gasp, but before she could scream I put my hand on her mouth. "Don't worry," I said in a kind of loud stage-whisper. "It's Peter—I think we're all in trouble. Can you find a light?"

There was no electricity at Naurataka, but the bedrooms all had small battery-powered bedside lamps. Ruth knew where hers was, and switched it on. "Why, you're soaking wet!" she said. "Have you been in the sea?"

"No, I've been in a river, but it's a long story, and I can't go into it now. Can you get dressed and come with me to find Caval?"

She didn't waste time arguing or asking questions. She put on a shirt and a pair of slacks, and then went to the dressing-table and began brushing her hair. "Can the hair wait?" I said.

"Not really. I must be a frightful sight."

"Well, I don't think so. And you're nothing like the mess I am. I think we've got very little time, and we *must* talk to Caval."

She gave a little shrug, and put down the brush. "Have you got a torch?" I asked.

"Yes."

"I think I know how to get to Caval's rooms. Come on."

I remembered the way to the Caval wing from my previous visit, but we hadn't got there when we met Caval himself, dressed, and carrying a Mannlicher big-game rifle. He had raised it menacingly, when I shone the torch on us. "Friends," I said. "But I'm afraid there may be enemies not far away. Can we talk somewhere where we're not likely to be overheard?"

"Better go up to the room you slept in. It's at the end of the house. But I don't think there's anyone else here. I heard a sound of someone moving about, and came to investigate. I think it must have been you."

"Probably. But we'll go upstairs just the same."

Throughout my walk that part of my mind which was not occupied with immediate problems like rocks and waterfalls had been busy making contingency plans. Why the Nuevan Government, or the Nuevan Army—I had no means even of guessing which—had suddenly turned hostile to me I had no idea, but obviously one or other or both of them had turned extremely hostile. The reason *must* relate to the caves. I had reported the finding of a shot man there—*somebody* in power in Nueva must have urgent reasons for not wanting this to be known. Arrested and kept in custody, I should have been safely out of the way, at least until such time as the body could be removed, or other necessary—from his or their point of view—action taken. But I had escaped. In my telephone call to the Prime Minister I had said that Ruth Caval had been with me—there was no reason why I shouldn't. Ruth could be presumed to have told Caval. Adam was dead, and Captain Amos and his crew didn't matter. They had not entered the caves, and if it suited officialdom to say that I must have been mistaken, or have made up the whole story, they couldn't deny it, even if they wanted to believe me. Ruth and Caval were different. Caval would believe Ruth, he owned the caves, and he would also want to know what had happened to me.

The plan of action that seemed to me most practical was for

the three of us to go on board the *Grand Duchess* while it was still dark, and clear out. She was big to handle without a crew, but I was confident that I could manage her, and once at sea we could make for the U.S. Virgin Islands, or even for Florida, where we should be out of reach of the Nuevans and in touch with the U.S. authorities for Ruth, and with access to my own people in London for me.

I didn't attempt long explanations. I said that there was something gravely wrong in the caves, that on reporting it I had been arrested, and that I was very much afraid that it could be only a matter of hours before the Army or the police came to Naurataka to pick up Ruth and Caval.

In a matter of fact way, Ruth said, "I know there is something wrong. I can't be sure what it is, but Peter is right."

Caval said, "Yes, I too have suspected that there is something very wrong. But can you really handle a big schooner by yourself—or with only Ruth and me?"

"I think so. She's in regular use, so there's probably water on board. We'd better take some food, if you can get hold of anything quickly, papers and money—and get off at once."

"All my nice new clothes—that's my second wardrobe gone inside a week. Can I take just one of my suitcases?"

"If you can carry it. I shall have to carry food."

"Well, I'm going to try."

She went off, and Caval took me to the kitchen. There was no refrigerator, but there was a huge ice-box. "We get ice brought by sea from Fort James," he said—an odd example of the human mind's inconsequential priorities. He found a big sugar-sack, in which we put two cooked fowls from the ice-box, tins of butter and bacon—you can buy these in tins in the West Indies—and a big side of salt fish, the salted cod from the Grand Banks that the French call *morue*, which was once the staple diet of the islands. We also found and put in the sack some bags of flour and rice, a collection of yams and other vegetables, and various other oddments that seemed likely to come in handy. When full the sack was pretty heavy, but we were going downhill, and I thought that if I could get it on my shoulders I could manage it.

"I shall take the rifle," Caval said. "I'll go and get some ammunition for it. I've also got two revolvers—we might as well have those as well."

He went off, and I went up to my room to collect my shaving

73

things and a change of clothes. None of this took long, and the three of us met with our various belongings at the front door. It was not quite three o'clock.

Ruth had one suitcase—it was so heavy that I suspected it contained a number of books as well as clothes. But she knew that she had to manage it. Caval had rifle, bandolier, two revolvers, and two boxes of revolver-cartridges, as well as a small valise of personal kit. I relieved him of one of the revolvers, and put the cartridges in my sack. Then we set off.

Downhill as it was, we had a lot to carry, and I was thankful to get to the quay. There were no signs that anybody else was stirring in the night. The *Grand Duchess* was lying to a mooring about fifty yards from the quay, but the dinghy was there, secured to a ring-bolt. We got the kit in the dinghy, got in ourselves, and cast off. I didn't want the noise of the outboard, so used the oars for the short distance to the mooring. I was worried all along that there might be someone sleeping on board the schooner, but Caval said this was unlikely, and it turned out that she was unattended.

We carried our personal things up the boarding-ladder with us, but I left the heavy sack and Ruth's suitcase in the dinghy, while I considered what to do. The dinghy could be slung in davits from the stern, but at first I thought we'd tow her out instead of trying to get her up. There wasn't a lot of room, though, between the mooring, the quay and the beach, and I wasn't sure that we might not have to go about to get away from the bay. I didn't want the complications of a tow in the darkness, so I brought the dinghy aft and got the falls from the davits to her. There was an anchor winch forward, but there was no winch aft—the schooner was designed for manpower rather than for labour-saving devices. But there was a two-part purchase on the blocks of the davits, and with Ruth to help the dinghy came up easily enough.

Now it was time for the sails. I didn't dare to show a light by using a torch, and it was some job in the dark to work out how the sheets and halliards ran. Mercifully the sails had not been stowed, but simply furled. Remembering how Captain Amos had got off under the big staysail and a jib I thought I'd do the same, but there was less wind at night than there had been in the morning, and I was afraid of getting caught inshore without enough area of sail to get out. So I got the mainsail up as well as a jib and staysail before letting go of the mooring. With everything ready I asked Caval to stay forward to drop the mooring-line as soon as I called out. Leaving the mainsheet free I put Ruth on it, telling her to be ready to haul the moment I told her to. The sheet ran in blocks, and though it would have been too much for her in anything of a blow I thought that she could just about manage it in the light wind we had.

I let the staysail draw, the jib began to fill, and as soon as I felt the schooner start to come alive I called out to Caval to let go. He did so neatly, without any fumbling, and we were away.

My heart was in my mouth as we began to close the quay. Without the mainsail I doubt if we should have had enough power to clear it, but I got Ruth to haul on the sheet, the drive from the big sail came to the rescue, the schooner answered her helm sweetly, and we got off with about a dozen yards to spare. All I had to do now was to stand out to sea. There were no particular dangers, and I could start thinking about a course when Nueva was safely below the horizon. No one so far knew of our departure, and by the time the *Grand Duchess* was discovered missing we should be out of sight, with nothing on the trackless sea to suggest where we had gone. My chief need was to find out what the schooner had on board in the way of charts. I made her comfortable, and asked Ruth to take the wheel while I explored with Caval. The steering compass was an antique, with an oil-lamp for the binnacle. As the Nuevans never sailed at night if they could help it I wondered if there would be any oil in the lamp. But there was, and when I'd got it lit I told Ruth to keep going north-west.

Caval, of course, knew the schooner, though he had not been on board her much for some years. There was a chart-table and a sort of navigating-corner to one side of the companionway leading to the saloon, but it did not look much used. "Our sailors go to sea as boys, they get to know the islands, and they navigate by instinct and tradition," Caval said. "Amos can use a sextant, but he hardly ever does. You may find one in one of those drawers, but I really don't know." There was a sextant, but I couldn't find any navigation tables. There were, however, a few charts, small-scale charts showing most of the Caribbean islands, and a large-scale chart of the approaches to Fort James. There was a fine old brass chronometer mounted as ship's clock in the saloon. From my watch it seemed fairly accurate, but I had no means of knowing when it was last rated, or what its rating was.

The galley was a small deckhouse just forward of the mainmast. There was a jar of coffee beans in a locker and a hardwood pestle and mortar for grinding them, but not much else in the way of stores. "They bring fresh food for each trip," Caval explained. A paraffin stove was rusty and clearly unused, but there was a forty-gallon drum of paraffin, nearly full. I was glad to see this, for the schooner's only lighting was from paraffin lamps.

Such cooking as was done on board was on an iron cooking-pot or brazier, of the traditional West Indian design. There were three of these, and they stood on a big sand-tray, about four feet square. Over the sand-tray was a chimney-opening, with a galvanised iron chimney extending about three feet above the deckhouse roof. Fuel was wood and charcoal, and a small pile of cut wood and two sacks of charcoal were stacked neatly in one corner. "I think I'd better take over the galley," Caval said. "I've often used a cooking-pot as a boy, and I think I can still get one going. I don't know what would happen if we tried to light that stove—safer to stick to the sand-tray and the cooking pot. It wouldn't be a bad idea to boil a pan of water now, and make some coffee."

The pans were there all right, but when Caval went to draw water from the pump that supplied the galley sink we got a shock for only a trickle came. "The tanks are below and you can get at them from the hold," Caval said. "I think I remember where they are. You fill them through a pipe covered by a brass plate on deck, and unless you do it in harbour at Fort James, where there is a water-hose from the quay, it's a tiresome job, because you have to bring barrels alongside and pump from them. It looks as if the crew's been slack about it—they'd just bring water in bottles for themselves on an ordinary trip. We'd better go and have a look."

The hold could be entered from below through a narrow door in the bulkhead, secured by two strong planks of wood that dropped into iron holders, bolted through the bulkhead. It could also, of course, be entered through the hatch on deck, but I didn't want to unbatten the hatch. I lighted two hurricane lamps to save the batteries of our only torches, and we went below. The water tanks were simple affairs of galvanised iron, but well designed and strongly fitted, one to port and one to starboard. Each had a screw capped opening for a dipstick, and a notched wooden dipstick was clipped to the bulkhead against one of the tanks. We tried them both: one seemed virtually empty, the other had about an inch of water in it. "There's enough for coffee, anyway, and if we boil it well it ought to be all right," Caval said philosophically. "We'll just have to get some more."

He went back to the galley to get one of the cooking-pots going, and I went aft to see how Ruth was getting on. She had had no trouble, for the schooner was on a comfortable reach with a light, steady wind, and there was no problem about holding her. It was beginning to get light, but there wasn't quite enough light yet to see the compass plainly, so I left the binnacle-lamp burning. "There should be some coffee up soon," I said.

"Where are we going?" she asked.

"Well, that's a bit uncertain at the moment. We shall have to put in somewhere for water because we seem to have precious little on board, but where I haven't worked out yet. It can wait till daylight—every minute is taking us farther away from Nueva, and that's the main thing just now."

While Caval was working in the galley I got our sack and Ruth's suitcase out of the dinghy. I took the sack along to the galley, and found Caval standing over a cooking-pot on which a pan of water was boiling cheerfully. "I'll let it boil while I pound the coffee—I couldn't even guess when the tanks were last cleaned out," he said. He put the wooden mortar on the galley sole and shook in some beans from the tin. "I'm surprised that they're roasted—normally we just parch what we need on a tin pan on a cooking pot. That's why Nuevan coffee is always so good—one of the reasons, anyway. I suppose they roasted the beans to make coffee for you yesterday."

The heavy wooden pestle made short work of pounding the coffee beans to powder. "Hasn't the coffee-grinder got to Nueva yet?" I asked.

"I daresay it has in some of the modern houses in Fort James. But why should it? There's nothing to go wrong with a pestle and mortar, it makes a fine smooth powder, and I doubt if it's any more work than a hand-ground coffee mill. As for electrical machinery—well, a pestle and mortar are a lot cheaper than electricity, even if you have it."

I left him to get on with the coffee-making, and took Ruth's suitcase below, to the cabin she'd been allotted when we changed for our swim—it seemed several lifetimes ago.

77

Caval appeared at the wheel with a tray and three steaming mugs almost as soon as I got back on deck. "I took the precaution of bringing a few bottles of rum on board," he said. "Since we haven't got any milk, I've used rum instead—you may find it an improvement."

I took the wheel from Ruth to leave her hands free for the coffee. The schooner was going so sweetly that I found no difficulty in holding her with one hand, with my mug of coffee in the other. It was a wonderful moment after the strain of the night. The rum-laced coffee was as nectar-like as anything I'd ever tasted, and it put life into all of us. The sun was coming up out of the sea, and it would soon be hot, though the God-given trade wind keeps the Atlantic edge of the Caribbean tropics pleasantly fresh. I asked Ruth to turn out the binnacle-light, and then asked Caval for his views on where we should make for.

"There's not an immediate water-crisis—we've enough for a day or so if we're careful," he said. "But we're not really free agents until we can get more water on board. Do you think you can find the Oyster Islands? They're about 130 miles from Nueva, and they don't belong to Nueva. If they belong to anybody they still belong to the Dutch, but as they're uninhabited it doesn't matter much. They're a group of rocks rather than islands, but some of the larger ones are about half a mile long, and I know that at least two have water on them, because I've been there several times when I was young enough to go for camping expeditions. They were hide-outs for buccaneers in the old days, and the islets with water have coconut palms, and wild fruit trees—the descendants of trees planted by the buccaneers. We can get water there, and we could do with some coconuts and fresh fruit. But the problem will be to find them."

"If Ruth will take the wheel again, we'll have a look at the chart," I said.

The chart showed the Oyster Bank, and a chain of cays running some twenty miles in a semi-circle roughly north-east to south-west. They looked a horrible group to get close to if you didn't know exactly where you were. On the other hand there appeared to be deep water round the bank, and no great dangers in the approach to the group. We'd been going more or less north-west from Nueva since we started, and although the schooner didn't have a patent log, I reckoned that we'd probably been making between four and five knots. With neither chronometer nor navigation tables I couldn't hope to work out an exact position, but I could judge local noon by the ancient system of watching shortening and lengthening shadows on deck, and if I took a series of sextant sights each side of noon I could interpolate what would not be far-off a noon-sight, and I could get a rough idea of latitude. Seventeenth- and eighteenth-century seamen were navigating these waters long before they could work out longitude, and my sextant, even if I didn't know the index error, was still a better instrument than the old back-staff they used.

I scaled off distances on the chart. Caval's 130 miles was a little short—the group of islets were more like 145 miles from Nueva, or at least from Naurataka. If we could keep up five knots, that was twenty-nine hours' sailing, of which we'd already done some three hours, more or less in the right direction. Our course should be NNW rather than north-west, and we could make a start on that straight away. The vital thing was to start a working log, making sure that our actual compass course was entered every quarter of an hour, so that the dead-reckoning we'd have mainly to rely on should be as accurate as possible. If the weather didn't blow up or otherwise upset my calculations, we should be safe enough making NNW for the next twenty-four hours, though it might be wise to heave-to for the last hours of darkness tomorrow morning, to avoid the consequences of any miscalculation which might bring us near the Oyster Rocks too soon.

"Yes, I think we can make your Oyster Bank all right," I said to Caval.

"Well, I'm not much good on a boat—the forest is more my line. But I can use a cooking-pot. I'll have a meal ready for us about eleven."

I went back to the wheel to set our new course, and to relieve Ruth. "Your suitcase is in the cabin where you changed for swimming," I said. "Caval's taken on the galley, and he's promised us a Nuevan breakfast around eleven. You're relieved till then. You can have a wash if you like, but it will have to be in sea water. There's a bucket with a line to it in the galley."

She went off. I settled the sheets for our new course, and realised suddenly how tired I was. I'd been up all night on a gruelling night-march, and I'd been taut with anxiety about getting the schooner to sea. I wanted desperately to go to sleep, but I couldn't turn in yet. I wanted to try for a noon-sight, and

79

if Ruth was going to be relief helmsman she had got to get some rest. Caval had done splendidly for a man in his late seventies, and if he was going to take on the galley I'd have to try not to use him for watch-keeping as well. The early morning sunshine and the wind on my cheek were soporific, and I nearly fell asleep at the wheel. Then I shook myself. This wouldn't do at all. The best way to keep awake was to do some hard thinking—it certainly needed to be done.

As soon as I began to think of it, the readiness of Ruth and Caval to abandon Naurataka and to accept my suggestion of a long voyage on an under-manned schooner seemed extraordinary. What did they know that I didn't? My mind went back to the moment when I'd uncovered the face of the dead man in the cave, and I had a sharp recollection of Ruth's gasp—"Oh no, Oh no, Oh no." Shock at seeing a human face mutilated by a bullet wound in the temple? Possible. But it was also possible that the shock was the face itself—that she recognised the face. She'd recovered quickly enough, but there were a lot of things that she needed to explain.

And why was Caval up and dressed, and armed with that formidable Mannlicher? Did he normally investigate slight noises in his own house, among his own people, with the Mannlicher? Could there be anything in his idea that the earthquake which destroyed Chacarima House had really been a bomb intended to remove him? I didn't see how it could have been a bomb—at least, it wasn't like any explosion that I'd ever come across before. But I wasn't an explosives expert, and short of expert examination of the ruins—if there were such experts on Nueva—there seemed no way of getting any further. Caval undoubtedly believed that someone was after him. But who? And why?

VI

THE BLACK NOTEBOOK

THE REST OF that day went more like a holiday cruise than the attempt of three fugitives to escape. Caval turned out a remarkably good breakfast of rice and salt fish, garnished with fried bananas. I reckoned that my watch was right within a minute or two, and when it said a quarter to twelve I started taking sun-sights. I wedged a belaying-pin as vertically as I could in a patch of clear sunshine on deck, and watched its shadow closely. It didn't shorten as noticeably as I could have wished, but it did shorten gradually, and I got Ruth to keep an eye on it while I took sights. I went on taking sights until my watch said that it was a quarter past twelve, and Ruth agreed that the shadow was definitely lengthening. I took the mean of my series of sights, and got a latitude which seemed at least not wildly improbable.

The *Grand Duchess* didn't seem to have a log—Captain Amos presumably knew his sea so well that he had no need of such refinements. I made a makeshift log with a plank and a measured length of line, and we'd been heaving it at intervals. It gave us speeds varying between four and a half and five and a half knots, so an average around five knots seemed reasonably likely. I guessed a longitude from our course and presumed speed, and marked a position on the chart. I had no confidence in its accuracy, and my dead reckoning was likely to be very rough indeed because I had no knowledge of tidal streams or currents, and no experience of the leeway that the schooner normally made. However, even a roughly guessed position was better than none, and I could hope for a check on our latitude if I could get a sight of Polaris at night.

I'd temporarily forgotten that Ruth was a mathematician, and was mildly surprised at the interest she took in my calculations until I remembered it. "My sort of navigation is by guess and by God," I said. "Maybe you can do some really elegant work with spherical trigonometry from first principles."

She laughed. "Maybe we can pick up a secondhand computer on the Oyster Rocks! As for finding the rocks—well, I think we'll have to leave it to your guesswork and such Divine aid as we can get."

I wasn't greatly worried about finding the rocks, though I was a bit bothered about the possibility of coming on them in the dark. The chart showed the Oyster Bank extending over some twenty miles, and several of the rocks or rocky islets rose to over 300 feet, so they should be visible for a considerable distance. Nothing could happen during the rest of the day, at any rate. I asked Ruth if she thought she could carry on till six p.m., and she said she could. "If there's any change in the wind, or the sails seem uncomfortable, call me at once," I said. "Try to keep her heading about 330 degrees. If she falls off more than a couple of degrees each side of 330, make a note of the time and the duration of the change."

I wanted to ask her a lot of questions, but I was too tired. I couldn't do anything about the answers, anyway, and I might be able to think straighter after a few hours' sleep.

As I lay down on my bunk I felt something bulky in my pocket, and pulled out the black notebook that I'd picked up in the cave. It had no name. About half the pages were still blank, and the rest were filled with figures and mathematical symbols. I could make neither head nor tail of any of it. I put it in my holdall with my shaving things, and went to sleep.

I had four hours of really refreshing sleep, and woke just after five. I felt tousled, and went on deck for a bucket of sea water. Ruth seemed quite happy at the helm. "There's been very little change in anything," she said. "She wanted to go a bit north— about 340 degrees—for nearly an hour between three and four o'clock, but I wrote down the time, and then she was all right again at 330."

"Fine. I'm going to have a wash, and then I'll relieve you."

I not only washed, but managed a shave as well. I don't pretend that shaving in cold sea-water is either pleasant or efficient, but if you have a sharp razor-blade it can be done. I've contrived to do it in the North Sea, and the tropical Atlantic provided kindlier sea water than the North Sea. I felt much better for the removal of a day and a half's growth of stubble, and went on deck mentally and physically better equipped for my next spell on watch. As it happened, I didn't relieve Ruth at once, for Caval appeared with a bottle of rum and three glasses.

"We can have a civilised drink before it gets dark," he said. "I've made some supper. I'm afraid it's rice again, but I've roasted some yams to go with it. Let's have a drink first, and then we can have supper before dark."

"We can be more civilised than that," I said. "We've a fair supply of paraffin, and I don't see why you and Ruth shouldn't sit down properly in the saloon. I can eat at the wheel all right. I'm all for a drink now, and I'll get the saloon lamp and the navigation lights going before I relieve Ruth. Then I'll carry on till midnight."

"I can probably manage to steer," Caval said. "We can break up the night between the three of us."

"No. It's far better to have a cook who's not mixed up with watch-keeping. Ruth and I can manage the watches, for the time being, anyway, and if you can rustle up some coffee around dawn it'll be much more valuable than taking a watch." I was concerned for the old man, and to relieve the cook of watch-keeping is good sea-practice in any case.

I enjoyed Caval's rum, and then made my round of the lamps. The saloon lamp was trimmed and three-parts full of oil, but the navigation lights obviously had not been used for ages. However, they only needed oil and a bit of cleaning, and by sunset I could report, "Lights burning brightly, and all well."

"You've done splendidly," I said to Ruth. "How are you feeling?"

"A bit stiff. But I've got much more used to the wheel, and I rather enjoy steering. I don't know what I'd do, though, if the wind suddenly went round and the sails were taken aback."

"Let the schooner do what she wants, and scream for me," I said. "It's not very likely to happen with this wind—it's more likely just to fall off for a bit, and then she'll roll and the sails slat. I'd notice any change like that, though, even if I were asleep, and I'd probably be on deck almost as soon as you could call out. Can you take over again at midnight?"

"Yes. But I'm not so sure about waking up."

"Don't worry. There's a handy lashing for the wheel, and I'll call you when the time comes. You'll get more rest if you can go to sleep without feeling that you've got to force yourself to wake up."

Caval called up from the saloon that supper was ready, and Ruth went below. They left the saloon door open, and the soft glow of lamplight from the companionway was homely and comforting. Ruth was back in a minute or two with a bowl of Caval's rice mixture for me, and I was ready enough for it. When she offered me a second helping, I was ready for that, too. Then she turned in. Caval tidied up his galley, and wished me a good night.

I was not sorry to be alone on deck. I shut the saloon door so that the light would not interfere with the binnacle, and settled down for my night watch. The schooner almost steered herself—she needed only a finger-touch on the wheel to stay on course. I could have added to her speed by setting another jib, and she seemed to have provision for a topsail, though we hadn't carried one on the trip to the Chacarima Inlet, and I hadn't worked out precisely how to set it—I didn't even know if there was such a sail on board. But I didn't want more sail. The schooner was comfortable and going well, and I had no intention of racing for the Oyster Rocks.

About halfway through my watch I got a good sight of Polaris, and felt reasonably confident about our north-south position. Our position east and west was another matter, but I was no worse off than any old-time mariner running down his latitude to try to get where he wanted. I was, in fact, a good deal better off, for I had at any rate some Admiralty charts of the area, and knew what to look out for. I decided to try to stop thinking about Chacarima caves for the moment, and to concentrate on finding Caval's islet with water on it in the Oyster group. When we'd filled up with water I should have to work out what to do, but the immediate task was to get water.

It was blissfully peaceful to be alone at the schooner's wheel in the clear tropical night. The wind remained steady, but had fallen off a bit with the coming of night, and I doubted if we were making more than about four knots. I had contemplated heaving to for the last hours of darkness in case we came too quickly to the Oyster Bank, but at our present speed we couldn't possibly make it, and the few miles extra northing we had made during Ruth's watch had also to be made up. So I decided to keep on sailing through the night.

Midnight came, but I didn't call Ruth. After my good sleep in the afternoon I wasn't feeling particularly tired, and I thought that she probably needed rest more than I did. So I let her sleep on until two o'clock, leaving her a relatively short watch until dawn. She was rather cross when I did call her, saying that I wasn't playing fair, but the fact that she needed to be woken up suggested that I was right in my feeling that she needed sleep.

I went below soon after two a.m. but I didn't turn in at once. I wanted to transfer my Polaris sight to the chart, and thought I might as well work up the notes on course and estimated speed that I'd made in my pocket diary, which served as our working log. In the diary was the note that Ruth had given me about our divergence in the afternoon from my set course of 330 degrees to around 340 degrees. It was a page torn from a little loose-leaf notebook, and I'd slipped it in the diary to work up later. I'd not seen her writing before, but as I looked at her neat, clear figures they seemed vaguely familiar, particularly an exceptionally neat 3, with a straight top-stroke like that of a printed 3. Suddenly I remembered where I'd seen that 3 recently. I got the black notebook from my holdall, and there it was. I put Ruth's navigational note against a page of the notebook from the Chacarima cave. The notebook was almost all figures and so was Ruth's navigational note, the figures of degrees and times. The handwritings were astonishingly similar, if not identical. What the hell could that mean?

My first thought was to take the black notebook to Ruth at once, and tackle her about it. But then I thought, No—we've got to get to the Oyster Bank for water, and Ruth is an essential member of the crew. I must wait until we've anchored safely and got water on board. There's got to be straight talking with both Ruth and Caval, but there's nothing to be gained by trying to do it now. Patience, as Cervantes observed somewhere—Patience, and shuffle the cards.

It wasn't easy to be patient, but I forced patience on myself. I tidied up the chart, and went to my bunk, taking the black notebook and Ruth's navigational note with me.

I had a hurricane lamp in my cabin, and its light was good enough to read by. I compared the figures on the note and in the notebook again, and was more than ever sure that they were in the same hand. There were twenty-three pages of figures in the notebook, a few of them crossed out as if they were false starts at proving something, the rest line after line of numbers, algebraical letters, and mathematical signs. There were some sets of what looked liked complex equations, but what any of them meant was beyond me. I pored over them for an hour and then gave up, turned out the lamp and tried to go to sleep. I couldn't get to sleep properly, but dozed off and on until half-past five. I'd left some sea water in a jug, so I got up, and had a quick wash, and went on deck.

It wasn't dawn yet, but the eastern sky was lightening. There was a steersman's bench behind the wheel, to allow the man at the helm to take the weight off his feet, but Ruth wasn't sitting on it. She was standing most responsibly at the wheel, silhouetted against the lightening sky. I thought what an attractive figure she made, and was at once cross with myself—she'd been up to some very funny business, and it was my job to find out what it was. That she happened to be an attractive woman was entirely irrelevant.

She was glad to see me, and called out gaily, "Morning, Peter. It's really rather lovely up here at night, and my watch has gone pretty quickly."

"Course still all right?" I asked.

"Yes, I think so. I've been down to about 327 and up to about 333. I jotted them down for you, with the times, but you'll see that they just about cancel out, and the average course must by very close to 330."

"Good. Steering a sailing boat is not like steering a liner, and you are doing well if you can hold a course within five degrees or so. This wonderful trade wind helps, but even so you'll soon promote yourself from deckhand to AB—that's Able-Bodied Seaman, in case you don't know."

"D.Phil., AB—sounds good."

"Don't swank. Do you know what an Able Seaman has to be competent to do?"

"Not exactly."

"Well, he has to be able to hand and reef a sail, to box the compass, and to steer."

"I can do the compass, and you said my steering was O.K."

"On a clear night in an easy wind. What happens if I send you up the mast to reef a topsail?"

"I just do my best, I suppose."

I couldn't help liking her, whatever she was up to.

"You'd better learn the Law of the Sea." I quoted the old Shipmaster's Rule.

Six days shalt thou labour, and do all that thou art able,
On the seventh, holystone the deck and scrape the cable.

"Pah. I'm going to join the Seaman's Union. They can deal with brutal blue-nosed skippers like you."

A few minutes after six Caval appeared with coffee. "I've found a tin of dried milk," he said, "so you can have milk this morning, if you want it. For myself, I shall stick to rum. There's a ration of two bananas apiece—that's the last of the bananas I put in our sack. If you can find Oyster Island there should be some wild ones growing there. When do you think we're likely to hit the island?"

"Hit it? Never, I hope. But we ought to be there soon after midday, and see it some time this morning. I'd like to get a bit more sail up. There's a yard on the foremast that looks as if it's meant for a square topsail. Do you know if there's such a sail on board?"

"I don't. But you're right, these schooners do carry a topsail sometimes. If the *Grand Duchess* has one, I expect it will be on board—there's really nowhere else to keep it. What sort of state it will be in is another matter."

"We can find out. I'll go and hunt in the sail locker."

The sail locker was forward, reached through a hatch in the foredeck just abaft the forecastle. It was light now, and the open hatch let in plenty of light. The locker was really a small hold. There were several sails on racks, but they were not tidily stowed —clearly the *Grand Duchess* kept her working suit furled and ready for use, and did not often carry more canvas. But I liked the look of the yard, and wanted to experiment with it. I also thought I'd get up another jib.

There was a spare mainsail, old and much patched, and I hunted through the rest of the considerably mixed bunch. I found a high-cut jib of the sort old sailors used to call a "Yankee", and after much pushing and pulling I dragged out what looked like a squaresail. All the sails were of heavy canvas, and it was a job to get my two sails up the hatch. With some help from Caval I managed it, and I opened the sails on deck. I could set the Yankee easily enough, but I didn't know my way about the squaresail.

Everything about the *Grand Duchess* was heavy and built to last, and there were strong tarred ratlines leading up both masts. I went up the foremast to have a look at the yard. It was a fine spar, but heavy, and I felt the need of a crew. However, I studied the blocks, worked out how they ran, and climbed down again to release the halliards. Then I lowered the yard and bent the topsail to it. I wasn't at all sure how the sheets went, but I devised a rig that worked, though I don't know even now if it was what the original rigger intended.

I had no experience of trimming square rig, but by a process of trial and error I got the sail setting fairly comfortably. It was a fine sight, and a grand powerful sail, with real drive in it. Trimmed as well as I could fix it, and sheeted home, I reckoned that it added at least half a knot to our speed. Then I got up the Yankee. That was a good sail, too, and suited the schooner. With the Yankee and the topsail up I heaved the log, and was delighted to find that we were doing between six and seven knots. The wind might have picked up a bit with dawn, but not much: our new speed was almost all due to the extra area of sail.

It made the schooner slightly more difficult to control, and Ruth was having a rather anxious time at the wheel when I relieved her. "I don't like that big square thing," she said, pointing to the topsail.

"You'll soon get used to it. It's a fine sail, and I'm sure the old schooner hands swore by it. But it does really want a crew, and I won't leave it up at night. For the moment it's doing well, helping to get us to our fresh water and bananas. Now you go and get some sleep. By the Nuevan breakfast time we ought to be in sight of our island."

All landfalls, even if you've only crossed the Channel from Dover to Calais, have a touch of miracle about them: it seems superhuman to have found your way across the pathless sea to the place to which you actually wanted to go. The best of modern navigational aids do not make the event less miraculous. What mariners of the ancient world must have felt when they made Tyre, or Carthage, or Corinth, I don't know—I suspect that they had the same sense of mingled triumph, humility, and gratitude to providence that I have whenever a buoy, or rock or headland comes up roughly where I have expected it to be. To make the Oyster Bank from Nueva was not really very difficult: I had compass and chart, a well-rigged schooner and a reliable wind. Even so, when one of the steep northern outliers of the Bank turned indisputably from cloud into land-mass I felt an enormous relief. We were a bit north of the point I'd been aiming for—roughly the middle of the bank—but I was no more than a few miles out, and it didn't matter, because with the wind steady from the north-east we could make southing without difficulty.

When the rock was unmistakable, and the line of other islets was beginning to appear, I called Caval from the galley. "There are your Oyster Islands," I said. "Can you tell me anything about the look of the one you used to go to?"

He peered ahead. "Your eyes are younger and better than mine," he said. "But yes, I can make out the islands. I'm afraid it is many years since I have been there. Let me think—they're a coral formation, and we anchored off a beach in a half-moon-shaped lagoon. The island rose quite steeply, and was well-wooded—only two or three of the group have trees, the rest are just bare rock. That would help to identify it. I remember rocks and islets stretching away on both sides, so it would be somewhere towards the middle of the group, I suppose."

"We ought to be able to find it. Can you take the wheel for a moment while I go below for the chart?"

I had the chart pretty well in my mind, but I wanted to make sure of the approach. The scale of the chart was too small to show much of individual islets, but the general picture was clear enough. The Bank was steep-to and there seemed no great hazards in the way. We could stand in safely to a mile or so offshore and then cruise gently along the group until we found a well-wooded island rising from a lagoon. If it had trees it would have water—it wouldn't much matter if it wasn't the actual camping island of Caval's youth.

Instead of being pleased at coming to the islands, Caval seemed profoundly unhappy. "I can't help thinking about Adam," he said. "He and I were about the same age, and we grew up together. Of course he was one of the servants and I was the young master, but that didn't make any difference. I don't really think it ever did. It was a feudal relationship, I suppose, but it was a happy one for both of us. And I sent him to his death."

89

"You didn't," I said sharply. "You sent him to accompany your guests on what should have been a perfectly ordinary picnic. You couldn't know what we were going to find in the cave, nor how it was going to affect him."

"I should have known that—fear of the caves is deeply rooted in all our people.... But you are right, and I must not be morbid. I can't help feeling horribly responsible, though.... Well, the psychologists talk of work as therapy—I'll get on with cooking the breakfast."

Going south, we made a spanking pace through the water, and it wasn't long before we were coasting the line of rocks and islets. They were an enchanting picture—azure sea, white coral beaches at the foot of the rocks. All the northerly ones seemed bare of vegetation, but as we passed one big and rather forbidding fellow that stood out a bit from the rest I could see the green of trees.

We were carrying too much sail for inshore navigation—the drive of the big topsail was an embarrassment now. I put the schooner into the wind, and trusted her to look after herself while I hurriedly took down the topsail and got in the Yankee jib. The clatter woke Ruth, and as I was getting back on course under the more handleable working rig she came on deck. "Oh, how beautiful!" she said.

I was glad to have her, for I wanted to go up the foremast to have a look at things, and to try to work out pilotage. We were safely past the big rock, but we had drifted inshore while I was handling the sails, and were now only about half a mile from the wooded island. From the crosstrees on the mast I could see a lagoon plainly. The northern arm of the enclosing beach terminated in a reef, but the reef didn't go the whole way across and there was an entrance a good couple of cables in width. Coming down from the mast I dropped the mainsail, and left Ruth at the helm to steer for the entrance under staysail and jib, while I went forward to see to the anchor. There was no problem about letting it go, but I was nervous about the manpower available for the antique winch when it came to getting the anchor up. However, we'd tackle that problem when we came to it.

Leaving the anchor ready to let go, I went back aft to Ruth. I told her to carry on as she was until I raised my arm, which meant that she was to turn into the wind. Then I went forward to the anchor.

We glided through the entrance, and I decided to make for the reef-end of the lagoon, where the shoreline cliffs and the reef itself offered considerable protection from the prevailing wind. The water was glass-clear, and I could see right to the bottom. There were a few coral-heads on the sand, with rainbow-coloured fish darting among them, but none of the corals came near enough to the surface to be dangerous.

I raised my arm. Ruth put the wheel hard over, the schooner came on the wind and lost way quickly. Just before we began to go astern I let go the anchor. It bit quickly, and we came to rest gently in about six fathoms.

We had our breakfast-lunch—rice, salt fish and a few peppers— on deck before going ashore. There was a certain sameness about Caval's cooking, but his readiness to take over the galley was a godsend, and he was sadly limited in raw materials. It was a magical anchorage. The sky-blue water of the lagoon curled away to the reef at one end, and to a low, palm-fringed promontory at the other. Ashore, the white coral beach rose to a green hill, the dark tropical green broken here and there by patches of vivid primary colours from some flowering tree or shrub.

"Yes, I think this must be the island," Caval said. "If I'm right a little river flows into the lagoon at the far end—you can't see it from here because of that clump of coconut trees. A few yards up the river there's a small waterfall. We used to have fresh water baths in the pool below it, and of course the water from the fall is pure spring-water, uncontaminated by the tide, or anything. Above the fall is the remains of an old plantation, where we should find some bananas and things."

"The problem is going to be to get the water on board," I said. "We don't seem to have much in the way of containers. There's an old barrel in the galley—it probably leaks, but I daresay it will take up when the wood gets wet. I wonder if we could fix up one of the pumps to pump water from the barrel in the dinghy into the tanks. I'll have a go, anyway."

There was a pump to get water from the tanks to the galley sink. The two tanks in the hold were connected by a pipe. I managed to undo this at one end, and to attach the hose normally

91

used for filling the schooner's tanks from a stand-pipe on a quay. Fortunately there was a fair length of hose, and if I could get this to the barrel we could pump water to the galley tap. With the dinghy brought alongside amidships, there was enough hose and to spare. If we cut it, there would be sufficient hose to run from the galley tap to the water-point on deck provided for piping water to the tanks. Having worked out that all this could be done, I decided not to cut the hose until we'd got a barrel of water alongside. The next job was to investigate the stream.

I launched the dinghy from the davits, and got the barrel down to her by a sling attached to the main halliard. As we could find only one four-gallon can of petrol for the outboard I decided not to use the motor, but to row ashore. The three of us got into the dinghy with the empty barrel, and a variety of jugs with which to fill the barrel, and set off.

We found the stream, just as Caval remembered it, and got the dinghy to within half a dozen yards of the waterfall. Filling the barrel with our jugs was an excessively tiresome job. The barrel held around forty gallons, and our biggest jug held about half a gallon. It wasn't practicable to get the dinghy right up to the fall, so every jugful meant a trip ashore. After a dozen such trips, using three jugs, we had about ten gallons of water in the barrel.

Then I had an idea: why not use the cut end of the hose? It would reach from the dinghy to the fall, and with luck would just pipe water into the barrel. Leaving Caval and Ruth I rowed back to the schooner, cut off a length of hose, and rowed back. It worked splendidly, and we had the barrel full in a few minutes.

A gallon of water weighs ten pounds, so the full barrel added some 400 pounds to the dinghy's weight. There seemed no point in carrying passengers as well, and as I thought I could manage the pumping on my own Caval and Ruth went off to explore the old plantation while I ferried the barrel back to the schooner.

My pumping-system was a bit tiresome at first, because of air in the hose, but at last I got the pump to suck, and after that it was plain sailing: the pump brought water to the galley tap, and a hose from the tap to the water-point on deck sent it below to the tanks. They were sixty-gallon tanks, and three barrel loads would fill them.

It wasn't quick work because of all the ferrying, and each

round trip took about an hour. But it got done, and when I'd emptied the third barrel I slung the barrel back on board and went back for a cargo of Ruth and Caval's foraging. They'd done remarkably well. They got four huge bunches of bananas, several dozen oranges and a nice pile of limes. Caval had hoped for yams or sweet potatoes, but there didn't seem to be any. There were, however, masses of coconuts. On Caval's advice we ignored those that had fallen, and picked the ripest fresh from the palms. Caval showed me how to climb a coconut palm by making a loop of a rope end, putting it round my ankles, and going up the trunk on the grip of the rope: you put your arms round the trunk, lifted your feet in the rope, gripped the trunk with the rope, and then did it again. It was just like going upstairs.

We ferried two dinghy-loads of fruit and coconuts out to the schooner, and with this substantial addition to our stores we felt well enough provisioned for anything. By this time it was late in the afternoon, and there seemed no point in setting sail again forthwith. By staying in our anchorage we could also get a full night's sleep, and depart in the morning, with the light of a whole day instead of an approaching night ahead of us. Caval was rather tired, but insisted that he would look after our supper. Leaving him to get on with this in his own time, Ruth and I went back to the beach for a walk ashore.

Instead of going to the river end of the beach we walked straight up it, first on sand, then through a fringe of coconut palm, and then, as the ground rose and became more soil than sand, we met much denser bush. There was no sort of path, but by sticking to the edge of the bush and walking under the coconuts where the going wasn't too bad we got to the foot of a rocky slope that led up to the highest point of the island. Here there was less vegetation, and by scrambling round and over the rocks we reached the summit.

It wasn't in any sense a mountaineering feat; the walk took about ten minutes, and I doubt if the crest was more than 350 feet or so above sea level. But it was our peak, and we could see over the whole island, perhaps half a mile across at its widest part and about three-quarters of a mile long. The *Grand Duchess* looked like a schooner on a picture postcard, peacefully at anchor in her blue lagoon, and nicely sheltered by the enclosing reef. Waves were breaking on the outer edge of the reef, but the lagoon itself was still, with only miniature wavelets coming to the beach. The faithful dinghy drawn up on the sand had the homely look of a friendly dog.

There was about an hour of daylight left, and as the descent would take only a few minutes there was no need to hurry back. We sat on a rock, enjoying the view and the sense of unbroken peace only to be found, perhaps, on an uninhabited island.

"By the way," I said, "I think I've got something of yours." I took the black notebook from my pocket and gave it to her.

VII

THE MAN IN THE CAVE

I DON'T KNOW what I expected to happen, but whatever it was I didn't expect her to throw her arms round my neck and burst into tears. "Is it never going to end?" she sobbed. "Oh, Peter, tell me what to do."

I was conscious of the fragrance of her hair, no scent that I could identify, but a warm fragrance that seemed to mingle the sun and the sea and the hibiscus flowering in the bush. I disengaged myself as well as I could, surprised to find her hands quite cold, in sharp contrast with the sun in her hair. "It might help if you told me a bit more of the truth," I said.

It was late afternoon, but it was still the tropics, and in spite of the tropics she shivered slightly. She said nothing, and I went on rather brutally, "I think you know a good deal about the dead man in the cave. Is he your former husband?"

"Charles? If only it were!" She gave a bitter little laugh. "Whose side are you on?"

"I didn't know there were sides to be on. I appear to be a fugitive from the Nuevan Army, and I think it quite likely that they're after you and Edward Caval as well. Since we've escaped together, you can take it that I'm with you for the moment. I can't say any more, because I don't know what you're talking about."

"Poor Peter. And you only came to Nueva to sell guns!" She paused for a minute. "Or did you come only to sell guns? There's something very odd about you. Why are you so close to the Prime Minister?"

"I'm not at all close to the Prime Minister. His Government invited me to Nueva as a technical representative of the British Government to discuss the re-equipment of the Nuevan Army. It's purely official business, and naturally I've discussed it with Mr Li Cook."

95

"Suppose we both tell each other the truth. You don't believe me, and I don't wholly believe you."

I got up. She stayed sitting, or rather huddled, on the rock, looking pathetically waif-like. "My dear Ruth, I didn't say I don't believe you, but only that I don't think you have told me the whole truth," I said. "There was no reason for you to tell me about your marriage, and the telephone call to your apartment about earthquakes. Your affairs are nothing to do with me, but if you do want to discuss them you shouldn't go out of your way to mislead me. You said, for instance, that you thought the voice on the telephone was your ex-husband's, somewhat disguised. But if you are divorced, and had not seen your husband since you left him, how on earth did he know about your trip to Nueva? And I think you did recognise the voice, and knew quite well that it was not your husband's."

"Peter, you talk like a policeman. Are you a policeman?"

I didn't answer, and she went on, "All right, I suppose I haven't been quite fair. But I've been so worried I don't know what to do. And I don't know who to trust, except poor old Mr Caval. I think I trust him. If I trust you, are you going to let me down, and hurt me, and perhaps Mr Caval as well?"

"I don't go about trying to hurt people. A few minutes ago you asked me to help you. I'm perfectly ready to help you if I can, but I can't help if I don't know what the trouble is."

She seemed to take a decision. "Well, I'm going to trust you. But you must sit down. I can't talk looking up at you."

I returned to the rock beside her. She didn't look at me, but at her hands in her lap, squeezed together tightly. "Everything I told you about my marriage is true, except that I didn't tell you more than the hundredth part of the hell I went through. I told you about Charles's infidelities—I didn't tell you about his twisted politics and totally unscrupulous attitude to life. I think I did tell you that as a physicist he is very able—I suppose that's why the university kept him on, in spite of various scandals. Or partly that, and partly that they were afraid of the political trouble he'd cause on the campus if they tried to sack him. Ostensibly Charles is ultra-Left, a Neo-Maoist-Dynamist, or something; in fact he's as amoral politically as in every other way, and about as utterly selfish as a human being can get. He felt it strengthened his hand to have an ultra-Left following, but that's all.

96

"I met his father a couple of times—very like Charles, except that he doesn't have Charles's scientific ability. They both have one obsession—to get their hands on Edward Caval's land. Charles used to talk about it quite openly—in his view they had a natural right to it because of the old grant from Charles II. Even before I really knew much about him I thought it a bit odd 'for an ultra-Left socialist to want to benefit from a Royalist grant of three centuries ago. When I did know more about him I was just sickened.

"It's true that I've never met Charles after I walked out, but it's not true that I didn't know of some of the things he was up to. That's because of Phil Grover—the research student I told you about, whose work Charles pinched. I told you that the boy came to me about it. I couldn't do anything for him, except tell him to report the facts to the Dean of Studies, which he didn't do, but I think it helped him a bit just to talk to me. Anyway, this boy was working on seismological theory, and about a year after I'd left Charles he wrote to me to ask if I could help him with the mathematics of some ideas he had. Well, it wasn't my business, but I felt that he'd been shabbily treated by Charles, and if I could do something for him it seemed to make it better, somehow. And I can't help being interested in any real mathematical problem. So I said he could come to see me. Do you know anything about seismology?"

"I told you I didn't."

"Well, I just wondered—that was one of the things I wondered about concerning you. I can't give a seismological lecture now—I'm not a seismologist myself, anyhow, only a mathematician. But basically, it's like this. The earth's crust is built up of a series of rock platforms, of different ages and structure, resting on one another like a child's building blocks. They've been there a long time, the rock-masses and counter-balancing pressures are enormous, and normally they're in a state of equilibrium.

"Now it can happen that sometimes one rock platform begins to slide over another—it may be that the angle is too steep for stability, or there may be some natural lubricant present, like graphite, or it may be that some upheaval far down in the earth has altered the pressure system, there's an almost infinite number of possible causes for a rock slide. But the effect of a rock slide is a tremor on the surface of the earth, and if the slide goes on, an earthquake. Phil Grover was working on a theory trying

97

to identify the conditions making for instability in the rock structure under any given area, and to use them to promote an earthquake where it wouldn't matter, or in a place from which people could be evacuated. You see, a rock slide has got to stop somewhere, and if you can make it happen when you want it to instead of waiting for an earthquake, you can let off the pressures under more or less controlled conditions, and allow the area concerned to regain stability.

"Actually to do any of this you've got to have two things—engineering technique capable of moving the masses concerned where and when you want to, and a mathematical technique capable of determining where and when to apply the engineering. Phil, who is essentially an engineering-physicist, reckoned that he'd gone a long way towards solving the engineering problems, but he was stuck over the maths. I needn't tell you that it's a most formidable mathematical problem, and although it may be possible to solve it theoretically, I think now that the practical application of any possible solution is at best extremely limited. But I'm getting ahead too fast. I was interested in Phil's problem at the time, a bit flattered, I suppose, that he'd come to me, and I spent months trying to work out a way of calculating all the things he wanted. That black notebook has some of my calculations. The dead man in the cave is Phil."

She spoke in a matter-of-fact way as if she were lecturing to a class. She had been so intent on trying to explain things, and I'd been so intent in listening to her, that both of us forgot the time. It was now quite dark. I took her hands, still cold, in mine, and kissed her lightly on the top of her head. "Thank you," I said. "You need have no fear of my not believing you now, and you need have no doubt about my being on your side. There's a great deal more that you must tell me, and there's a great deal of work to be done, as quickly as we can do it. But we can't stay here. Poor old Caval will be sick with worry, and we must get back to the schooner."

She obeyed like a child, without saying anything, and like a child kept her hand in mine as we walked back to the beach. It was rough going in the dark, but it wasn't far, and as soon as we were out of the shadow of the trees the combination of slight moon and starlight was enough to indicate the outline of the dinghy on the beach. A faint light from the schooner's portholes showed where she lay, and I enjoyed the physical relief of rowing out to her. Caval met us at the gangway. "Thank God you've come," he said. "I was wondering whether I ought to try to swim ashore to look for you. And I've caught some fish, and made a really decent supper."

"We owe you a lot of explanation, and I think you owe us a bit of explanation, too," I said. "But it can wait. We all need that supper of yours, and as far as I'm concerned I need some of your rum. Ruth, too, could do with a good stiff drink."

"It's all ready in the saloon," Caval said.

I ought to have paid more attention to Caval's cooking. It was enterprising of him to fish for our supper, and I'm sure it was an admirable meal, but I have to admit that I have absolutely no recollection of what we ate. There was far too much sorting out to do. I was beginning to get a glimmering of the really nasty work that was going on in Nueva, and angry at being used, or so it seemed to me, as an expendable pawn in it. But I was not angry with either Ruth or old Caval.

"Have you told Mr Caval that you recognised the dead man in the cave?" I asked Ruth as soon as the rum was poured out.

"Yes."

"I suppose that is why you were both so ready to come with me when I turned up out of the night."

"Only partly so," Caval said. "We felt a considerable responsibility for you." He was oddly impressive, the authority of a lifetime, indeed of generations of Cavals, making him a kind of natural chairman of our small meeting.

"Do you know of the experiments in artificial earthquakes?" I asked.

Ruth answered. "He knows what I've told you, and he knows a bit more that I haven't yet had time to tell you. It would make things clearer if I went on where we left off on the island."

"Please do."

"Well, I told you that I tried to work out mathematical solutions for Phil's problems. I was so interested in the maths that I didn't think of anything else for quite some time. When I did, I got more and more puzzled. Why had Phil come to me? He had a research job at a great university, he had access to a first-class team of mathematicians, served by high-grade computers and all the rest of it. Why come to me?

"Most of our dealings were by letter, but he used to visit me

99

from time to time, to come up with new problems, or to ask about something I'd sent him that he hadn't quite understood. When I began wondering what it was all about, I asked him point blank why he wasn't using the university's research staff. I didn't like his answer. He said, 'But you know I'm still working with Charles'.

"I didn't know, and honestly, it hadn't even occurred to me. It didn't seem possible that a man who'd had some of his own work stolen by Charles should have gone on working with him. I asked him why, and he wouldn't tell me, except to say that I must know how able Charles was in his own line. Well, I knew that Charles's line wasn't seismology. It was nuclear physics, and although it could obviously be related to earth structures, Charles had never, so far as I knew, taken any particular interest in earthquakes. I was on quite good terms with Phil, and I tried to question him without his really knowing it. I didn't get very far, except to feel that Charles had some hold over him which he wasn't prepared to tell me about. And to realise that whatever Charles was up to it wasn't any good.

"Then I did a lot of hard thinking for myself, and I realised that the possibility of being able to cause earthquakes, even over a limited area, had a number of military implications, and that some governments might be ready to pay out a great deal of money for the process. I thought of going to our own U.S. Government about it, but I didn't know anyone to go to, and then I thought of something else: if Charles was going to sell out to some foreign government he might find himself in a tricky position. And he had a lot of notes in my handwriting, and letters to Phil with my name on—I'd never thought of being secretive about anything. If there was trouble over selling secrets to a foreign power, or misusing the facilities of an American university in the interests of a foreign power, all he had to do was to disappear and leave Phil and me to carry the can.

"I got more and more frightened. I told Phil I'd done all I could and that I didn't have time for any more, I moved to a new job, got a new address, and although one or two more letters from Phil were forwarded to me, I didn't reply to them.

"I told you that I'd had a letter from Mr Caval inviting me to Nueva. That was true, but I didn't tell you that I'd written to him first. You see, I didn't know who to go to for advice. My own parents are dead, I'd spent so much time working for my

D.Phil. and working to keep myself while I studied, that I didn't have any close friends. I suppose that was one of the reasons why I fell for Charles. From what he'd told me of the Cavals I knew that there was a senior member of the family who didn't seem a bit like Charles or his father, and since this was in a sense a Caval matter, I wrote to Edward Caval and asked if he could give me advice on a matter concerning the family."

"I thought she wanted money," Caval said. "I told you that I'd had a lot of inquiries made about Charles, in the course of which I learned about his marriage to Ruth, his treatment of her, and their divorce. It seemed to me that she'd been treated shamefully, and if she needed some financial help I was prepared to give it. So I replied inviting her to Nueva, and paying her fare. I tell you this now, because it was what I thought then. Since meeting Ruth I can but offer her the most abject apology."

"The telephone call—who really made it?" I asked.

"There wasn't any telephone call. I made it up for your benefit. I didn't know who you were, or what you were doing in Nueva. I wanted to test your reaction to the prediction of earthquakes, and I had to have some reason for thinking about it."

I was a little pleased. At least my feeling that there was something wrong about that telephone call was right.

I suppose we finished supper. I have a vague recollection of Caval's bringing us some coffee, and a sharp recollection of his saying, "That's why I wrote to Sir Edmund Pusey."

"What did you say to him?" I asked.

"I couldn't tell him much, and over the past year or so I've not been absolutely sure of the integrity of my mail. But I was deeply worried by Ruth's story—whatever it was, it was far more than a matter for Nueva, and it might concern the whole balance of military power in the world. So I wrote a chatty, personal letter, saying that I was reading the Bible more as I grew old and was particularly impressed by I Corinthians 10, verses 11 and 12.* I trusted him to read between my lines, look up Corinthians 10 and respond. He did. He sent you."

"So I was right. You're not quite what you seem," Ruth said.

* Now these things happened unto them by way of example, and they were written for our admonition, upon whom the ends of the ages are come. Wherefore let him that thinketh he standeth take heed lest he fall.

I ignored this. How like Sir Edmund, I thought bitterly, to send me out to Nueva without telling me anything about Caval! Then I thought that I wasn't being quite fair—Pusey had no idea *why* Caval had written to him, he knew that I should meet Caval, and, in his customary way, he had left me a free hand to act as circumstances might suggest. Instead of suggesting anything they'd forced a lot of action that none of us could have foreseen. What mattered now was to decide what to do next.

"When you wrote to Pusey," I said, "you knew Ruth's story, but did you have any idea that any of Charles's lot would be coming to Nueva?"

"No. And I didn't think on those lines until after the earthquake at Chacarima—some time after the earthquake, in fact, for when you and Ruth went back to Fort James I had no idea that it wasn't a perfectly natural earthquake. Now I'm quite sure that it wasn't—I think it was some sort of experiment, with the double purpose of trying to get rid of me. And what you found in the caves strongly suggests that whatever is going on is directed from there. But why was the young man killed?"

"I think I know why he was killed," Ruth said. "At least, the notebook that you found suggests a possible reason. You see, there's an error in those figures. I didn't realise it when I gave them to Phil, but I discovered it later and told him about it. Whatever crooked work Phil was mixed up in he was a scientist first, and he would have told people about the error. That wouldn't have suited Charles—if he was out to sell an artificial earthquake process, he wouldn't want anyone to know that it was incomplete and might not work at all. Charles probably reckoned that he had nothing to fear from me, and that Phil was the only person who knew about the mistake."

"If the Chacarima earthquake was artificially produced it couldn't have been a very serious mistake," I said. "If that was an artificial earthquake, then the process does work."

"No, it's not like that." Ruth shook her head impatiently—it was hard to explain rarefied mathematics to people whose maths more or less ended with the multiplication table. "It's not a mistake in the ordinary sense, it's more a fallacy in mathematical logic. I can't go into it all now, but roughly it means that a process which *may* work over a relatively short distance, won't have the same effect if the distance is extended. It also means that the process *may* have a kind of reciprocal effect—it may work backwards, as it were. Oh, I can't explain." She put her head in her hands.

"Don't worry about it now—obviously it matters tremendously in any real assessment of the process, but to anyone trying to bluff the sale of the process it doesn't matter at all," I said. "Do you know what sort of machinery is needed for the engineering side of the process?"

"I don't. Phil never explained in any detail, and in a way I wasn't greatly interested, because I was concerned solely with the maths. It required the generation and transmission of a special sort of radio wave along the plane between rock surfaces to a point mathematically determined beforehand—that's where the maths came in—at which the magnetic forces in the wave would bring about a kind of nuclear explosion. I don't know enough about nuclear physics to understand the ins and outs of the explosion—I do know that it wasn't any ordinary sort of atomic explosion, but in some way a limited one, designed to make one rock-mass slide on another and so produce an earthquake. I don't know how well the radio-explosion would work. I do know that the maths wouldn't work at all reliably."

"Something worked at Chacarima. So they'd need a generator and a fair amount of radio equipment. We don't know how much, but we can assume that it would be fairly heavy." I turned to Caval. "How difficult would it be to instal heavy equipment somewhere in the caves?" I asked.

"By sea, not all that difficult—there's deep water a long way into the hillside. The chief problem would be to unload it, but there's no reason why a crane or gantry shouldn't be set up to deal with it. I know of one place where it could be done quite easily. Instead of going ashore where you did you carry on by boat for about another half-mile, and you come to a wide cavern with a firm rock floor. That light we saw from Naurataka was almost certainly a ship going to the inlet—there could have been several previous ships which I wouldn't have known about, because you can't see them from Chacarima House."

"It seems to me that we ought to go back to investigate. We don't know what's going on in the caves, but we do know that something is going on, and the killing of the young physicist suggests that it is something pretty urgent. And the extraordinary business in arresting me has further implications—that nothing must come out about murder in the caves until some deal or other

103

has been completed. There isn't time to get in touch with London or Washington, and on what we know at present I don't see what either the British or the U.S. Government could do. We *must* find out more. With luck I should be able to get in and out of the caves without being arrested. But we *must* keep control of the schooner. Is there anywhere we can lie up with a reasonable chance of not being seen for twenty-four hours or so?"

Caval considered "There's the bay on the other side of the headland forming one shore of the Chacarima Inlet," he said. "No one goes there much, and the bay itself extends almost into the bush. From there, we can get into the caves by climbing the headland—I say 'we' because you couldn't possibly find the way on your own. But I know those caves from boyhood—they're a honeycomb of passages, and I *think* I can get to the place where machinery is most probably installed without going near the inlet. We can but try, anyway."

I did a hurried calculation. "We must go into the bay when it's dark, which means some time during tomorrow night," I said. "I think we can just about make it, but it means starting now, and doing without our comfortable night at anchor."

Tired as they were, both Ruth and the old man were marvellous. I needed them both at the ancient winch to get up the anchor, but mercifully it had bitten in clean sand, and wasn't snagged on some coral-head. We had to go about to clear the entrance, but there was plenty of room in the lagoon, and once we were away from the half-reef that sheltered our anchorage there was a clean wind to take us out to sea. We had come about NNW from Nueva, and the way back was more or less SSE, a fine point of sailing for the generally NE tradewind. As before, the wind seemed to have fallen off a bit at night, and I wished I could set the big squaresail. But I didn't want to tackle it in the dark, and reckoned that if I got it up at dawn we'd have ample power to make the run back to Nueva in time to get there in the small hours of the following morning. As soon as I'd settled the *Grand Duchess* on her course, I persuaded Ruth and Caval to turn in. Ruth demurred at first, saying that I'd had a heavy day with all the water-ferrying, and that she would take the night watch. But I was too worked up for sleep, and thought I'd do better to get some rest next day. In the end we compromised. I said I'd carry on until two a.m. and then call Ruth to take the watch until dawn. I wanted to be up at dawn anyway, to get the squaresail set.

Alone at the wheel, I tried to make sense of all that I'd learned. Poor Ruth, she hadn't had much of a life. I could understand her falling for Charles. Presumably he had his share of the undoubted Caval charm, his Nuevan background adding a romantic touch to his real ability as a scientist. Ruth, on her first holiday for years, exhausted by struggling for her D.Phil., must have thought she was the happiest woman in the world, with a distinguished husband and a fine academic life awaiting her. What a vile awakening! It seemed to me that she had acted with determined courage, accepting that her only course was to draw a firm line across the ledger of her life and open a new page. Why had she then got mixed up with Phil Grover? Conceivably he had been attracted to her, but she hadn't talked as if she were at all attached to him. She had been shocked to find him dead, but she didn't appear to have suffered any great emotional shock —rather, she had assessed his death in a cool, analytical way as part of the problem of her ex-husband's scheming. Perhaps she had told the simple truth when she said that she felt that she could make up a little for Charles's treatment of the boy.

What was Charles up to, and why had Phil Grover gone to Nueva? Was Charles there too? It seemed quite likely. Was there anything in the artificial earthquake process? It sounded like science fiction—but so would the idea of putting men on the moon a few years ago. Chacarima House had certainly been destroyed by some sort of earthquake, and by all accounts it was a distinctly unusual earthquake, extremely limited in area, and with none of the accompanying physical features that Nuevan earthquakes are supposed to have. One could dismiss the Carib story as bush-myth—but the Caribs had been living with earthquakes for a long time, and their folklore, based on generations of acute observation, might well have something in it. The Carib man had said that whatever destroyed Chacarima House had emanated from the Chacarima caves. He put it down to the river's anger, but that was a natural relation of cause and effect in primitive thinking. Had the Caribs seen ships going to the caves and wondered what was going on? I wished that there was time to go into their forest territory. They trusted Caval, and perhaps they would talk to him. But there wasn't time. If we were to uncover the secret of the caves, we'd have to do it ourselves.

Suppose it was possible to set up equipment at Point A and cause an earthquake at Point B—the Chacarima caves would seem an ideal site for an earthquake control centre. I thought again of the map of the North Atlantic, and of the strategic value of the Chacarima Inlet—uninterrupted sea reaching to the populous eastern shores of the United States, and to much of western Europe. I didn't know anything about the seismology of the Atlantic seabed, but it might be easier to send those diabolical radio waves along the structures of an ocean floor than under some land-mass. I shivered as the thought came to me. If the process worked, or even if people could be made to think it worked, whoever controlled the process and the Chacarima caves could hold a large part of the world to ransom.

But who was involved? Was the Nuevan Government going it alone? It seemed unlikely, for though Nuevan control of the caves might threaten other people with destruction, the island had scarcely the resources to exploit a threat to the rest of the world. But Nueva in partnership with some Great Power—that would be a very different matter.

How far had negotiations—if there were any negotiations—gone? The killing of Phil Grover suggested that they were not yet finalised, that his knowledge of a fallacy in the process could upset things. That assumed, of course, that Ruth was right, and that Grover had been killed because he knew too much about the process. He might have been killed for some quite unrelated reason, personal jealousy, a quarrel over a woman—there were a myriad possibilities. But assuming that the rest of our speculation was on the right lines, Ruth's idea made sense. Anybody wanting to use or to develop the process would not have killed Grover—his work was far too valuable. If he knew that the process was incomplete, and nothing like as reliable as it might be made out to be, then anyone trying to sell the process had a powerful motive for his murder.

What could I hope to do by going back to Nueva? Find out what was happening in the caves? With luck, I could do that perhaps. But what then? The Nuevan Government was apparently after me, and if I were seen in Nueva God alone knew what would happen to me. I might be able to get away in the schooner with knowledge that might be vital to my own Government and its allies, but whether the *Grand Duchess* could escape a naval search was another matter. The main point in our favour was that unless we were seen nobody could know that we were anywhere near Nueva; and at sea the good old *Duchess*, for all her grand name, was humble and inconspicuous enough. But it was taking an appalling risk—and it was risk to Caval and Ruth as well as to me. Had I any right to expose them to such risk? Ought I not to change course now and make for the U.S. Virgin Islands where they would be safe?

This disturbing thought was interrupted by Ruth herself. "It's well after two o'clock and you never called me," she said. "If you are really on my side you have got to keep your promises."

"What's worrying me is whether I have any right to take you and Edward Caval back to Nueva. I have only to change course and you can soon be safe in U.S. territory."

"And let whatever evil is going on in those caves just go on going on?"

"Is it any of your business? There may be very great danger—and in any case we may not be able to achieve anything."

"Peter, you need to get some sleep. Give me the wheel. I've already seen the compass, and I'm going to stay on this course."

VIII

JOURNEY UNDERGROUND

WE RAISED THE high central ridge of Nueva with still a couple of hours of daylight left. The old *Duchess* had done us proud. She'd had a soldier's wind and she'd tramped along like a Guardsman hour after hour. The big squaresail which I'd set at dawn was like a powerhouse aloft, and there were long periods when I reckoned that she was making a good ten knots.

Much as I disliked the thought of entering an unknown bay in darkness, I didn't want to close the coast by daylight in case anybody spotted us. I didn't think it was all that likely, but I'd no idea what we were up against, and it would be silly to take any avoidable risk. I got the squaresail and the mainsail off her, and also took in the powerful Yankee. With one staysail up we reduced speed to little over a knot, and pottered towards the island. The main problem was to find the bay, but we were helped here by the fairly easily identifiable mass of the big headland that enclosed it. I aimed to get near enough to the coast by daylight to identify the headland and take bearings, and then to wait far enough offshore to be hull down to any watcher. When it was properly dark, we would go in.

I still had misgivings about what we were doing. I had put my feelings to Ruth again, and to Caval, when we met for breakfast—there was still plenty of time to alter course and bear away for safety and the U.S. Virgins. Neither would contemplate any turning back. Ruth said, "When you talked about this before, you asked if it was any of my business. Well, I think it is—they're using a lot of my maths in whatever it is they're doing, and I want to know what it is. Whether we can stop them is another matter, but at least we should try to get some facts to report to Washington, or to Peter's London."

Caval said, "They're my caves, and I can't help feeling a personal responsibility for whatever they are being used for. And there's Adam's death—he wouldn't have died if you hadn't come across the murdered man. Whoever committed that murder is largely responsible for Adam's death. I'd like to see whoever it was brought to justice. He can't be tried for Adam's death, of course, but he can be tried for the other murder."

So that was that, and we carried on to Nueva.

When the short tropical twilight came I got up the mainsail and another jib—that gave us plenty of power for what we had to do. The chart was encouraging as far as it went. As long as we kept away from the headland there were no off-lying dangers, and there seemed to be a least depth of six fathoms well into the bay. What I wasn't clear about was just how far this relatively deep water extended—I wanted if possible to get up to the fringing bush before anchoring, so that the schooner would be hidden to some extent, and at least not visible in silhouette or moonlight in the open bay. But that would have to be dealt with when we got there.

It was a pity that Caval had never been greatly interested in boats—he knew and understood the bush, and the configuration of the bay, but things like tidal reach and least depths had not much concerned him. He thought that the bush-shore of the bay was steep-to—there was no beach as there was on the other side of the headland, but he had no idea of how much water there actually was.

The bay faced roughly east, which gave us a clean approach in a north-easterly wind. We glided in like a ghost-ship, and I carried on for a couple of cables before checking her. Then I handed all the headsails, and hung in the wind with the main free. There wasn't a lot of wind in the comparative shelter of the headland, but I thought that the mainsail would provide all the power we needed to glide gently towards the bush. With the sheet free, I gave the wheel to Ruth, telling her to harden the sheet just enough to get us moving when I called to her. Then I went forward with the leadline. I didn't dare to use a torch, but I'd marked the line with strips of cloth, which I could feel in the dark. With my first cast all seemed well—there was a good eight fathoms under us. I called to Ruth, the schooner collected herself, and we edged inshore. The floor of the bay seemed a reliable slight slope. I got two more casts of eight fathoms before it went to seven, and the seven-fathom line held for a good cable. The bay was narrowing now, or at least our end of it was, becoming a finger of water running into the bush. I could make out the shapes of trees, several of them taller than the schooner's masts. I let six fathoms go, then five. When the lead showed four I thought it was time to stop chancing our luck. The tide was somewhere near the last of the ebb, so we could rely on not losing much of our four fathoms. I let go the anchor cable, and we came to rest not more than thirty yards from the shore. As far as I could make out in the darkness we were well screened from anyone not directly watching from the bush in front of us. I set our big jib in stops, and left the mainsail only loosely furled, so that we could get away quickly. Then it was time to go ashore.

We'd had much discussion about what, exactly, we could aim to do. My object was simply to get into the caves, discover, if possible, just what was installed there, and then get out again to sail for U.S. territory with whatever information we could gather. Caval would have to come with me, because he knew the caves, and an entrance from the cliff which, he said, would take us through the honeycomb of passages to the main cavern entered from the sea. I hoped he could find the way. I did not want Ruth with us—two was enough for an exploring party, and a third could only add to the hazards of a tricky journey in the dark, and to the possibilities of being spotted if there was anyone in the caves to spot us. Ruth, however, jibbed at this, and she was supported by Caval. "What do I do if anything happens to you and you don't come back?" she said. "I can't sail the schooner by myself—and I can't know how long to wait for you, whether to go ashore and try to look for you, or what. If we're together, at least we all know what is happening. Besides, neither of you knows anything at all of the sort of apparatus that may be there. I can't pretend that I know much, but I do know a bit about what it has to do, and I might be able to make sense of something that you couldn't."

Caval was not greatly impressed by this argument, but he was very much concerned about Ruth's safety. "She doesn't know the island: if she had to go ashore and try to get anywhere, the Lord alone knows what might happen to her," he said. I thought that she'd probably be safer on the schooner than anywhere else —there was plenty of food and water on board, and if the worst came to the worst and we didn't turn up all she had to do was to stay there until someone spotted her. But I did accept that this would be a harrowing prospect for her, and rather against my own judgment, I accepted that she'd better come with us.

We travelled lightly. Caval insisted on taking his Mannlicher rifle, which I thought unnecessary, but he said he was used to it and would feel happier to have it with him. Ruth and I took the two revolvers—"Though I've never fired a gun," she said.

"A gun is either a smooth-bore firearm or a piece of artillery," I rebuked her. "Only illiterates call revolvers guns."

"Well, you'd better keep out of the way if I have to use it."

Having no bread we could manage nothing in the way of sandwiches, but we took some coconut, and a piece of dried cod. Uncooked it looked repulsive, but it was dried and edible, and would keep us going for a bit if for any reason we got stuck in the caves. The *Grand Duchess*'s galley was not well off for picnic containers, but there were some empty bottles and I filled one of these with water. I also took one of the remaining full bottles of Caval's rum. We had two torches between us, and on Caval's advice we took a hurricane lamp. I also took a coil of line, which I slung over my shoulder.

Caval had been studying the shore, or as much of the general line of it as he could make out in the dark. "I don't think we want to go ashore here—it would be quite a long walk round the bay and it's rough going," he said. "If you could row back to the headland it would probably save time."

There was no problem about this. I launched the dinghy, and pulled away from the schooner.

Caval sat on the fore thwart, peering into the darkness. "Make for about the middle of the headland," he said. "I'll tell you when to go in."

It was an eerie little voyage. There was no sound but the slight plash of the oars, no light from anywhere ashore. It was just after nine o'clock, and after I'd been rowing for about twenty minutes Caval said, "Just beyond that clump of mangroves—it's not a good beach, but we can get ashore on some rocks; I don't suppose they've moved." I looked round, and, my eyes now used to the dark, I could see the mass of mangrove trees growing down into the water. I pulled round them, and into a little inlet that ended with a rocky patch of rather muddy beach. Caval, remarkably agile for his age, went ashore first, pulled us in with the painter, and held the dinghy for Ruth. I followed them, and hunted around for somewhere to make fast. It wasn't a good place for laying out the anchor, but by going back towards the mangroves I found a strong root to take the painter. She'd be safe enough here, I thought, and nicely screened by the mangrove trees.

"We've got to get about halfway up the cliff," Caval said. "There's no path, but it's more a steep scramble than a climb. Follow me."

I put Ruth between us, and brought up the rear. We did not go straight up the cliffside, but worked our way diagonally along it, heading seaward. There was certainly no path, but we were in a sort of narrow gulley, with bushes and trailing lianas to each side of us, but not much vegetation in the gulley itself. I thought we were probably in a watercourse, not a regular stream but a sort of *wadi* that took water from the hillside in the rainy season. It was quite dry now.

We had climbed for just under half an hour when Caval stopped—indeed, the *wadi* itself stopped, apparently coming to a dead end under a massive overhanging rock. Caval hunted round for a minute or two, and then suddenly vanished—one moment he was there, the next he wasn't. I put a hand on Ruth's shoulder. "Where on earth has he got to?" There was probably no one within a mile or two to hear me, but I found myself whispering—it was that sort of place. Ruth had been nearer to him. "He just walked into the hillside," she whispered back.

Then we heard Caval's voice, apparently coming out of the rock. "A little to your left," he said, "and you'll find a crack in the rock. You can just get through if you go sideways. It's quite safe."

Ruth held my hand as we followed the directions of the disembodied voice. We felt our way round the rock, and yes, there was a narrow gap. Ruth wriggled into it. "Are you all right?" I asked.

I heard her scrabbling for a moment, then "Fine now," she said. "You can stand up once you're through. Come on, Peter."

The crack in the rock wall was perhaps two yards long. It seemed horribly narrow, and I had to crouch sideways to get through. I had a stab of claustrophobic panic in the middle. Whether or not Ruth sensed this I don't know, but she put out her arm towards me and I was thankful to touch her fingers. Then I was standing beside her.

It had been dark outside, but compared with the utter blackness of the cavern we were in the memory of the night seemed brilliant. Something brushed my face, then another something, with a soft whirring sound. Ruth clung to me, shivering. "They're only bats," Caval said. "Quite harmless."

"Oh Peter, don't let them get in my hair," Ruth gasped.

I wasn't at all clear how to prevent bats from getting in anyone's hair, but I patted Ruth's head, which seemed to comfort her a bit. Then there was the sound of a match striking, and a sudden dazzling blaze as the flame came. "I'm going to light the lamp," Caval said. "We'd better save our torches. I don't think there is any danger of the lamp's being seen here—we're at least three-quarters of a mile from the sea part of the caves, and they're on a different level, anyway."

The lamp showed that we were in a long passage-cave, the floor rising steeply away from us. Like the caves through which Adam had taken us, it seemed immensely high—the light could not reach the roof. "The bats won't bother you now," Caval said.

"Thank Heaven for that," said Ruth.

Caval laughed. "The bats are one of the reasons why people are frightened of the caves," he said, "but they're only fruit-eating bats, not vampires. There are all sorts of legends about them, of course, but they live on wild fruits from the bush. They'd have a go at mangoes if there were a mango plantation, but there isn't, and they don't do anybody any harm. And they don't go far into the caves—they just live round about the entrances. So don't worry about them. We've got some way to go so we'd better start."

"All this is water-made, I suppose," I said.

"Yes, and in the rains we'd have difficulty in getting through—the way we came up becomes a river after heavy rain. We're quite safe now, though. And you'll find the passages easy walking, because they've all been smoothed by water."

Caval led on, and we followed in the same order as before, Ruth behind him, and I next to her. The passage climbed straight for a hundred yards or so, then forked. We took the right-hand fork, and, still climbing, seemed to be following a route rather like a corniche road, only we were inside the mountain. We plodded on steadily, and I became conscious of a noise, rather like a distant train. "That is the waterfall," Caval said. "We have got to pass behind it, and that is the only difficult bit—we have to get down to a lower level, and it's something of a scramble. Fortunately the rock here all seems quite dry."

The noise rapidly grew louder, and it was hard to hear anyone speak. Caval stopped, raised the lamp and held up his other hand as one halts traffic. There was an opening to the left which seemed to be another passage, but the path in front of us seemed to have become a hole in the ground. The lamplight didn't reach to the bottom, so I shone my torch. This revealed that the hole wasn't a vertical fall, but a steep jumble of broken rock. It was not an attractive descent, but looked possible. I shone my torch round the lip of the hole, and found a projecting rock in the wall of the cave along which we'd come. "I think we'd better use the line," I said, "and I think it might be helpful for me to go first, so that if either of you slip I have a chance of catching you."

The projecting rock was a good hold for the line. With Caval holding the lamp and Ruth shining the other torch, I went down gingerly. I put my own torch in my pocket, so that I had both hands free. The line was a great help, and I was soon at the bottom, where the cave-path seemed to continue, not climbing now, but more or less level. The rock-fall was a descent of perhaps thirty feet. I had plenty of line, and by holding up my end I could give it a clear run. I wanted Caval to send the lamp down the line, but I couldn't convey what I wanted because of the noise from the waterfall. The only thing was to go up again.

Caval and Ruth couldn't understand what was happening, and met me anxiously. "What's the matter?" Caval shouted into my ear.

"Nothing—the descent's not all that bad," I shouted back. "But we want the lamp down there, and it would be easier to send it on the line. I've come up to fix it."

He nodded. I ran my end of the line through the wire handle of the lamp, and there was enough line to cut off a section to make a check-line for letting down the lamp. "Hold the lamp until I get to the bottom," I said, "and when I raise my arm send down the lamp on the check line. The lamp at the bottom will give some light for you and Ruth, and I'll shine my torch upwards for you too."

As soon as I was sure that they both understood, I went down again, an easier trip this time because I knew what was in front of me. Our lamp-manoeuvre worked well. Ruth came down after the lamp, and Caval followed her, neither having any serious trouble. At the foot of the rock-fall we resumed our old positions, Caval leading, Ruth next, and I behind her. I took back the cut piece of line that we'd used for the lamp, but left the rest of it to hang from the projecting rock at the top—it would be handy if we had to come back this way.

The roar of water became deafening, and the cavern path began to be wet and rather slippery. Suddenly the whole of one side of the cave was water, a solid curtain of water falling from a cliff far above our heads. The falling water, hurled several yards over the lip of the cliff that made the waterfall, fell clear of our path—we were safely behind it. But the whole place was wet with spray thrown up from the foot of the fall. We pressed ourselves against the inside wall of the cave. To walk behind the waterfall was a terrifying passage in the lamplight, but I think it was not really very dangerous. The cave, scooped out of the rock by aeons of falling water, was quite spacious, and the floor against the inside wall was relatively dry. I doubt if the river that flowed over the unseen cliff was more than twenty yards wide, but in the dim light of one hurricane lamp the passage behind the waterfall seemed endless. When we had crossed we huddled together instinctively, Ruth putting her arms round me and clinging to me.

But we stopped only for a moment. Then Caval held up the lamp, signed to us to go on, and we continued our strange journey.

Gradually the noise of the fall got fainter, and when it was possible to speak without shouting Caval stopped, and turned out the lamp. "Look," he said. For a few seconds after the sudden extinguishing of the lamp I could see nothing. Then, as my eyes adjusted themselves, I could make out what he had seen because he had been half-expecting it—a faint light, more a lessening of the darkness, at the end of the passage ahead of us.

"I doubt if we can be heard, but we mustn't show any more light," he said. "About fifty yards on this cave runs into the great sea-cavern leading to the Chacarima Inlet—we come out in a sort of gallery, well above the floor of the sea-cave. That is where I'd expect to find radio or other installations, if there's anything to find. And it looks as if there is something, because of the light. It can't be from outside because we're much too far inside the caves, and in any case there isn't any light outside because it's night." I looked at my watch: it was just midnight.

Caval unslung his Mannlicher and went forward slowly. Ruth and I followed, side by side now, for there was plenty of room.

Our cave did not lead directly to the sea-cavern, but a side-opening to the left did. It was through this opening that a faint luminosity was coming, like the light at one end of a corridor from a lighted room at the other end. There was also a slight noise—the rhythmic hum of a dynamo.

Keeping close to the rock-wall, we edged round the corner, coming out, as Caval had said, on to a narrow platform that overhung the great sea-cavern like a gallery. There, a truly astonishing sight awaited us—we were looking down on a power station, or rather, a combination of power station and dock. The floor of the great cavern ended in a natural quay, and at the quay a small freighter of perhaps 400 tons was unloading. Several large machines were already installed in one part of the cave, and a man with a forklift truck was taking crates from the freighter to the machine area. A group of men round one machine were working round an opened crate. The whole place was well lighted, but fortunately for us the lights, on street-lamp standards, were all below our gallery.

The freighter was almost directly below us. Being broadside on I couldn't see her stern where her port of registry should have been displayed, but it might not have been there to be seen, for the name on her bow seemed to have been painted out. Two men were standing on the after-deck. I recognised one as the Prime Minister, Mr Li Cook. The other was a European. Ruth gave a little shuddering gasp, and I put my arm round her. Caval fingered his Mannlicher, but didn't do anything.

By some trick of acoustics in the cave we could hear every word the men were saying, as plainly as if we were standing beside them. The slight hum of the dynamo made no difference; it was constant and low pitched, and had become simply background noise.

"His Excellency is due here this afternoon," the European said.

"Then I shall meet him here," said the Prime Minister. "He should, I think, be much impressed."

"We've laid on a demonstration for him. It will have to be at sea, of course, but it won't be more than a couple of miles out, and should be clearly visible from the clifftop. There will be a sudden storm over a defined area, and probably a huge waterspout."

"Good. He is coming by sea, I suppose."

"Yes. He has chartered a big American yacht to pick him up in Jamaica, which he has been visiting as an ordinary tourist. We have had a radio message to say that she is on her way, and as far as we know on time. She should make Chacarima Inlet around four o'clock."

"And you think he is fully empowered to come to terms?"

"I'm sure of it. Can you imagine the Chinese letting such an opportunity slip out of their hands?"

"No. You have done very well. I shall need troops, of course, to establish my personal rule. I can't wholly rely on the Nuevan Army—too many of the Staff have been at Sandhurst or West Point."

"His Excellency understands that. You have simply to fix a date for Fort James to be occupied, and all will be arranged."

The Prime Minister looked at his watch. "Well, Charles, twenty-four hours from now, or perhaps a little less, I shall be the most powerful man in the world. You will have power, too, and everything else you want. There will be a few small diplomatic difficulties, no doubt—but with the power at our disposal, what can anyone do?"

"Are you staying here until His Excellency comes?"

"Yes. The cabin you have arranged for me seems very comfortable. Officially I left this morning on a private visit to Barbados, so I am not even in Nueva. Well, it's been a long day, and we need clear heads tomorrow. I wish you good night."

We watched the two of them go below, and then without a whisper to each other we slipped back into our own cave. When we were safely round the corner Caval lighted our lamp again and we went back the way we'd come. When we were past the waterfall, and far enough beyond it to be able to talk, Caval said, "I need a drink, and I think five minutes' rest."

"We all do." I got out the rum bottle, and since we had no cups I handed it to Caval. "You're the senior citizen, and anyway it's your rum," I said. "Ruth after you, then me."

Caval took a long swig and gave the bottle to Ruth, but she passed it to me. "I don't think I want any rum," she said. "I've got to think."

"So have I, and good rum helps thought." I took my turn at the bottle, and felt much better for it.

"I could have shot both of them without the least difficulty. Why didn't I?" Caval said.

"Because you're not a murderer, and because it wouldn't have done any good. Whoever is coming tomorrow would still come. What's the matter, Ruth?"

She'd shut her eyes, and the lamplight emphasised the strain and misery in her face. "I can't work it out," she said.

"Can't work what out?"

"The demonstration he talked about. Yes, I know he destroyed the house, and I daresay he thinks it will work again, but he killed Phil, and Phil knew much more about it than he does. Why did he kill Phil?"

"Because Phil knew too much."

"Yes, but it can't be quite like that. When I thought that I didn't know how far things had gone—I didn't know about all the equipment in the cave. He needed Phil."

"Perhaps Phil didn't like what he was doing, and was in a position to stop it."

"It may be something like that. But Charles sounded horribly confident, and he can't really be confident about it."

"All that family are gamblers," Caval said.

The psychology of the Antoine Cavals may have been enthralling to Ruth and Edward Caval, but I felt a sense of desperate urgency. "I'm afraid we've had our rest," I said. "There's very little time left."

"What are you going to do?" Caval asked.

"I've got a sort of plan. It may work or it may not, but I'd rather not talk about it now because I haven't thought out all the implications. It means getting to Fort James as soon as humanly possible."

"I thought we were going to make for one of the U.S. islands."

"That was before we knew what we know now. If we just sail for the U.S. Virgins the meeting will have taken place long before we get there, God knows what hellish alliance may be fixed up, and it may be too late to do anything about it. If we can get to Fort James, there's just a chance we may be able to stop it. Will you come with me to Fort James?"

"Peter's inclined to want to take over people," Ruth said. She was fighting hard to get back her old self-possession. "In this instance I'm game to trust him."

"Three against the world? Very well," Caval said.

I think I was more deeply moved than ever before in my life.

We made good progress on the journey back through the caves, for once we'd got up the rock-fall the rest of the way was downhill. Then came disaster—Caval slipped on some scree in the dried-up watercourse that led down to the sea, and fell heavily. When he tried to get up, he couldn't. "Something's happened to my left leg," he said. "I expect it's only a strain, and will pass off in a few minutes."

It didn't. We were trying not to show a light on the open hillside, but I had to use a torch now. As far as Ruth and I could make out there was nothing broken in the leg itself or in knee or ankle, but when he tried to stand, he just couldn't.

After the fourth try, he said, "It's no good, my children. You've got work to do, and as you said before there's precious little time. Leave me here. Perhaps you can come back for me later on. If not, or if the pain gets very bad, I've got my rifle. I've had a long and mostly good life, and I'm not in the least afraid of ending it. Indeed, I'd rather end it here, on my own land while it's still mine, than get in the way of what you're trying to do."

"It's a point of view," I said, "and an honourable one. But it isn't going to be like that. We haven't far to get down to the boat now, it's downhill and you're no great weight. Put your arms round my shoulders, and I'll get you up on my back. Ruth will stay close behind, to protect your leg, and hold you if you start slipping."

We were helped by the slope: getting down in front of him I got him up, put one arm under his good leg, and let the other dangle. I threw the Mannlicher into the scrub, also the hurricane lamp—we had to get rid of every ounce we could. The rest of the descent was horrible. Caval was not heavily built and he was old, but he must have weighed at least 130 pounds and he was a dreadful burden. And all the time I was afraid of slipping myself, perhaps injuring him more, or perhaps putting myself out of action. Ruth was splendid. She was carrying both torches, both revolvers, and the bag with our bits of food and bottles of rum and water, which it seemed folly to jettison in case we needed them. With all this, she helped to support Caval, moving step by step with me, and holding him on my back. It was an appalling journey, and just how we managed it I don't know, but we did.

When at last we got to the boat we all three took a swig of rum. Although he couldn't stand, Caval found that he could sit upright, and this helped us to get him into the boat. It was a glorious feeling to cast off and leave the blessed sea to take the weight of everything.

Back on the schooner I got a sling under Caval's arms and hauled him on board with the davits. We didn't try to get him below, but made him as comfortable as we could on deck.

Then came the problem of getting out of the bay. Until we cleared the headland we should have to beat, and I'd gone so far in towards the bush that there was virtually no wind to get us started.

I couldn't tow the schooner with the oars, but we had the dinghy's outboard and so far had used none of the fuel for it. Towing with the dinghy under power from the outboard ought to get the schooner moving. There would be the engine-noise, of course, but that couldn't be helped. We'd *got* to get to sea, and if there was anyone on shore within hearing distance of the outboard they could think what they liked.

Ruth and I got up the anchor and then I dropped down into the dinghy and started the engine. At rest the *Grand Duchess* was a ponderous old boat, and at first I wondered whether the engine really did have enough power to get her moving. But she had clean, fine lines, and slowly her head came round. Once she could follow at the end of the tow line instead of having to be dragged round she moved easily, and I didn't even have to use full throttle. I took her clear of the bay and the best part of half a mile out to sea before letting the line slacken and catching her boarding ladder as she came up.

Having left the headsails in stops, and the main only loosely furled, it didn't take long to get under way. I didn't try to get the dinghy up: I'd shipped the outboard before returning to the schooner so that there should be less drag, and—reversing roles—left the *Duchess* to tow her small but invaluable partner.

I took the wheel from Ruth as the sails filled and the schooner picked up speed. "Now we must decide where to go," I said.

It was a few minutes after four a.m.

IX

I GIVE MYSELF UP

W E C R O S S E D T H E mouth of the Chacarima Inlet without lights, but once we were well past I wanted the schooner to become respectable, so I handed the wheel to Ruth and lit our navigation lamps. Caval was sitting on deck, his back against the mainmast. I had put him on the windward side of the deck, so that the slight heel of the schooner tended to wedge him against the mast, and there was less risk of his slipping. I got him a rug and a couple of pillows, and he was quite happy to stay where he was—I didn't want to carry him below for fear of doing further damage to his leg.

The success or failure of my plan, such as it was, seemed to me to depend largely on the time I could get to Fort James—the earlier we could get there, the better chance we might have. The sea distance to Fort James was slightly less than by land, because we could sail direct, whereas the road had to follow the indentations of the coast. Even so, we had at least forty miles to go, and I couldn't bank on averaging more than five or six knots—something like eight hours' sailing. That would bring us to midday, much too late for what I wanted to try to do. The only real hope was to put in at some place where we could hire a car, and as we were sailing towards the most populous coast of Nueva this seemed reasonably practicable.

The chart offered a coastal village called Partika, about eight miles down the coast from Chacarima. It seemed to have a harbour of sorts, and I asked Caval what it was like. "It used to be a fishing village, but it has been considerably developed over the past few years," he said. "There is one big hotel, and several smaller ones. You should certainly be able to get a car there, and I can tell you just where to go. I had a houseboy called Elias who was good with cars, and was promoted to be a chauffeur. About five years ago I set him up in a small garage business at Partika. He's done very well, and if you find him he'd do everything he could for us."

That sounded like an answer to prayer, and I laid a course for Partika, which meant no more than closing the coast before reaching a headland which otherwise we should have had to clear. It gave us a rather better wind, and we were off the entrance to Partika harbour soon after five o'clock.

The harbour was unlighted—Neuvan coastal shipping being reluctant to sail at night—and, not knowing the entrance, I anchored in some ten fathoms in a place marked on the chart as Partika Roads. It had some shelter from a headland, but was about a quarter of a mile outside the harbour. I should have liked to get to a quay, but in the circumstances it couldn't be done. Ruth helped me to carry Caval aft, where I put a line under his arms again. Ruth then went down to the dinghy to receive him, and I lowered him gently to her. I threw some pillows into the dinghy, and she made him as comfortable as she could. The outboard took us ashore in a few minutes.

I made for a sandy beach at one end of the little harbour, jumped out in about a foot of water, and hauled in the dinghy. Leaving Ruth to stay with the dinghy I walked round a group of houses to the road, where, Caval said, I should find the Elias garage about a hundred yards along. It was getting light now, and at the garage there were signs of life. An elderly man was replacing a "Closed" sign by the garage's one petrol pump with a sign that said "Open".

"Can you please tell me where I can find Mr Elias?" I asked.

"Only one Elias here and that's me, sir," he replied in a friendly way.

"I have Mr Caval with me in a boat. He is hurt, and we need a car to get to Fort James. Can you help us, do you think?"

"Mr *Edward* Caval, sir?"

"Yes."

"Mr Edward give me my garage, sir. Get in this car, and we go now."

He pointed to a big Buick standing in the forecourt, and called out to someone in the huose to say that he was going to Fort James. Taking a turning that I hadn't noticed, he drove the car directly on to the beach, got out, and ran towards the boat. "Oh Mr Edward sir, they tell me you hurt!"

"Well, I seem to have damaged my leg somehow. Thank you, Elias, it is good of you to come."

"We get you to Fort James quick, sir, to best doctor in Nueva."

With Elias to help we soon had Caval out of the boat and in the car. Ruth, Elias and I then dragged the dinghy up the beach above the tide-line, where, Elias said, she could be left quite safely. Ruth got into the back of the car with Caval, and I sat in front beside Elias. I gave him Brigadier Ezra's address. He didn't question anything, just nodded. The brigadier lived in a good residential part of Fort James, and for all Elias knew we were going to the house of some friend where Caval could be put to bed.

I had been so keyed up with getting ashore at Partika that I hadn't thought of anything beyond finding transport to take us to Fort James. Now that we were on our way the full hopelessness of our position came back to me. I was staking everything on one remark that we'd overheard in the cave—the Prime Minister's observation that he could not wholly rely on the Nuevan Army. That might well be so—but was there the slightest chance that the Nuevan Army would be prepared to rely on me? And who was the Nuevan Army? My only real contact was with Brigadier Ezra. I'd liked him, and he'd appeared to like me, but that was when I was a distinguished official visitor. Now I was a fugitive on the run, whom the Nuevan Army had been ordered to arrest. Would he believe anything I said? Why should he? Well, whatever might happen to me, at least we could get Caval to hospital. And Ruth was an American citizen—we ought to be able to get some protection for her.

Thanks to the big car and Elias's driving, it was just half-past six when we reached the Brigadier's house. As before, he was sitting in his verandah, drinking coffee and eating a pineapple. Asking Caval and Ruth to stay in the car, I got out and walked up to him.

"Good Lord, Colonel, you look as if you've been living rough. Have you come to give yourself up?" He did not sound friendly.

"Not exactly," I said.

"You should not come armed." He was looking at the revolver in my belt. I'd completely forgotten about it. Ruth had been carrying it when we got Caval down the cliff, and I suppose I had just put it back in its holster.

"Sorry. You can have it, anyway." I put the revolver on the

table in front of him. "Can I talk to you for ten minutes? It is vitally important that you should listen to me. The whole independence of Nueva is at stake."

"You are very melodramatic. Who is in the car with you?"

"Mr Edward Caval, Mrs Ruth Caval, and a driver. Mr Caval is hurt. While I talk to you, may I ask the driver to take Mr Caval to hospital, and to bring Ruth Caval back here?"

"I must send an officer with them." He clapped his hands, and an orderly appeared. "Tell Captain Fernandes that I want him immediately," he said. Then, to me, "What do you want to say?"

"I'm not discussing anything in the intervals of giving orders to your servants. If this is going to be your attitude, Nueva can go to hell."

It was his turn to show a little embarrassment. He was saved having to say anything by the appearance of the captain—I learned later that the brigadier's house was next door to an Army establishment where there was always a detachment on duty, and that Captain Fernandes had not to come far.

Speaking rather more politely, the brigadier told the captain to accompany Mr Caval to hospital, to see him made comfortable, and then to return with Mrs Ruth Caval. When they'd gone, he turned to me. "I haven't got much time, but I'm prepared to listen to you for ten minutes."

"What I have to say is private. This is a very open verandah."

"Very well. Come into the house." He picked up my revolver, and stood back for me to walk into the house in front of him. We went to his study where he sat down at a desk. He did not invite me to sit down.

"Unless you are prepared, and able, to act at once, by this evening Nueva will no longer be independent, and you may expect the Nuevan Army to be disbanded," I said.

"What on earth do you mean?"

I gave him a hurried account of the artificial earthquake process, and of the Prime Minister's meeting in the cave. I went on, "As far as I can make out Mr Li Cook has arranged to do a deal with an emissary of the Chinese Government, who is due to meet him at Chacarima this afternoon. In return for giving the secret of the Chacarima caves to the Chinese, Mr Li Cook is asking for Chinese support to establish his personal dictatorship in Nueva. He seems to think that he can make himself the most powerful man in the world, but in this, of course, he must be mad, for obviously he will be no more than a Chinese puppet. The effects on Nueva you can work out for yourself."

The brigadier said nothing for a long minute. Then he said, "Your arrest was ordered on the ground that you were meeting agents of the American CIA at Chacarima to promote a Government more favourable to the American tourist industry than the present Nuevan Government. I was told that while your status as an officer of the British Ministry of Defence was authentic, your real purpose in persuading us to buy your new rifle was that the rifles should be available to CIA agents in Nueva. What have you to say to that?"

"If you believe that, you will believe anything. May I ask if this information about me came from your own intelligence sources?"

"As a matter of fact, it didn't. I was much surprised, and very much shocked, because to me you had seemed genuine enough. The Prime Minister has his own sources of information, and I have no reason to distrust them."

I began to despair. "Very well, then. Let events take their course. I regret only that I had faith in the patriotism of the Nuevan Army."

"You put me in a very difficult position. Suppose that what you say is even partly true?"

"It is not partly true. It is all true."

"But it can't be. You see, the Prime Minister is not even in Nueva at present. He is on a private visit to Barbados."

"He told people that he was going to Barbados, but he didn't go."

The brigadier picked up his telephone and asked for a number. While it was being got for him, he said, "I am taking you sufficiently seriously to speak to the guard commander at the airport. If he confirms that the Prime Minister left for Barbados yesterday, then obviously you are lying."

I had almost given up caring. I heard the brigadier talking into the telephone, but was too tired to take in the one-sided conversation. He was on the telephone for what seemed ages. When at last he put it down, he said, "We have an air force regiment. The commander is a close friend of mine, and I know all his officers. I have just had some curious information. The Prime Minister's private aircraft did take off for Barbados yesterday.

But it came back, and landed on an unused runway away from the main area of the airport. The officer on duty went at once to see if anything was wrong. He was told that the plane had returned because of a radio message which made the Prime Minister cancel his trip. He was told further that in no circumstances was his return to be reported—there were important reasons why it should not be disclosed. I have learned this only because the officer concerned is a personal friend. He has disobeyed orders in talking to me."

"But they were not orders given to him by his proper military superior."

"You have a point there. . . . Oh God, Colonel, what ought I to do?"

"Believe what I have said to you, and act on that belief. There is very little time."

He put his head in his hands. Then he got up, all trace of indecision gone, and held out his hand. "I'm sorry for the reception I gave you, but you must admit that your arrival and your story were both extremely puzzling," he said. "Here is your pistol—you may need it before the day is out. Now for that lecture on infantry tactics that you promised me."

We both laughed, I with a sense of infinite relief, he with a considerable edge of nervous tension.

"Thank you for trusting me—I realise the weight of responsibility you carry," I said. "As for tactics, the military problem is relatively simple. The real problem is how to deal with the Prime Minister. There, your judgment is better than mine because you know Nuevan politics and I don't. It seems obvious that you must be prepared to set up some form of provisional Government."

"The military problem first."

"Well, you can test my story easily enough by going into the Chacarima caves. But you must go in with a certain amount of strength. I saw no more than perhaps half a dozen men, but I should expect a guard on all that sensational equipment, and a battalion could hide up in those caves without the slightest difficulty. I doubt if there is anything like that, though—I should expect between ten and twenty armed men, determined gangsters rather than soldiers. But they are in a strong position, and it will need strength to flush them out. There is also the question of escape—you do not want anybody to escape. There is a great deal that we do not know, and you must try to hold everybody for questioning. There is only one road out of Chacarima, and you can block that on the high ground above the place. But remember my escape—you will want pickets widely extended on both sides of the road. Probably, though, there will be no attempt to get away by land. The small freighter there looked a powerful vessel, and I should expect them to try to get her out. So you will need a naval patrol in the Chacarima Inlet."

"Our navy consists of one old fishery protection boat given to us by the Royal Navy as a goodwill offering, and two or three motor launches."

"With good crews they should be enough. What armament does the fishery protection gunboat carry?"

"I don't know offhand. I doubt if she has anything bigger than one three-inch gun."

"The old naval three-inch is a powerful weapon—it would be enough to sink the freighter if necessary. Let's hope it doesn't come to that. There's another need for a naval force. The Chinese emissary is coming by sea, in a chartered American yacht. He ought to be intercepted."

"There'll be fearful international complications."

"There will, but as you have not been officially informed of the arrival of a Chinese envoy you can refuse to recognise him, and he can be deported without much fuss. The Chinese themselves are in no position to do anything. As long as you control the situation in Nueva, you can count on the blessing of the rest of the world. Can you count on your Army?"

"I can count on my own rifle regiment, and on the air force regiment. We have two batteries of gunners, some good signallers and engineers. Yes, I am sure we can count on the Army. I must call a Staff meeting straight away. The Chief of Staff, whom you met, is my superior and he will make difficulties, but he is a bit of a dodderer, and he is not really important. He may have to be put under house arrest. The rest of my colleagues will act with me, I think, when they understand the situation. Will you come with me to the Staff meeting?"

"I'm at your disposal for anything, Brigadier, but it would be much better for me not to. This is a Nuevan matter, I'm an outsider, and already under suspicion as a CIA agent. You can put that right, I hope, but you will do it more easily in my absence. How long will your meeting take?"

"It will take at least an hour to collect people, and I don't see how we can get through in less than an hour after that. After all, we are arranging a revolution."

"If you really want my advice, I think you must act now, before you have your meeting. Go ahead with the meeting by all means, but send two battalions to Chacarima now, and have the heights occupied this morning. And get the navy to sea. You need not give the naval commander detailed instructions yet, but say that he must have a force patrolling off the Chacarima Inlet by noon, to await orders. If you will introduce me to your battalion commanders I'll go with them to Chacarima if you like, and meet you there after you have had your meeting."

"All right. I've never taken part in a revolution before, and I suppose you can't do everything according to President's Regulations—actually, they're your own Queen's Regulations which we inherited and reprinted, with scarcely the change of a comma." He went to the telephone again, and made three calls in quick succession. "My own aide, Captain Theophilus, will be here in a moment," he said. "I'm going to send him with you. Lieutenant-Colonel Garcia and Lieutenant-Colonel Strong are also on their way—they are my two battalion commanders. When did you last have anything to eat?"

"I'm not particularly hungry, but I should love some coffee, and perhaps a couple of bananas."

"Right." He opened the study door and called his servant. While the coffee was being fetched, Ruth, accompanied by the young Captain Fernandes, came back. "I've a job for you, Fernandes," the brigadier said. "Collect a company of your men and transport for them, and go out on the Chacarima road to the place where it crosses the ridge above the Chacarima factory. You are to hold the road, and stop anybody travelling on it in either direction, whoever they are or say they are. Treat them with consideration, but detain them firmly until you get further orders."

"I understand, sir."

"Good. Then get out there just as soon as you possibly can. You can expect reinforcements some time later this morning."

The captain saluted, and went off.

The coffee came, and I poured a cup for Ruth. "Can we have another cup?" I asked.

"Of course." Never had coffee tasted better.

"The news about Mr Caval is not good," Ruth said. "It is the Caval hospital, incidentally—it seems that he provides most of the money for it. As soon as they realised that it really was Edward Caval everybody began running round to help him. He was X-rayed at once—he has a fractured hip, and I'm afraid there seem to be some complications. He has to have an operation, but they don't want to do it until he has rested a bit and been given some sort of emergency treatment. Meanwhile they've put him in a lovely room, and he has sent for various people—his Fort James agent, his lawyer, and a few others. The hospital rather disapproves, but you know Edward Caval—when he wants something done he gives orders, and that's that."

"I am sorry about his injury. He is a good man," the brigadier said. "You have not told me how he came to be injured."

"No, and it will have to wait. Your aide has come, I think, and another car's just arrived, too."

The brigadier sent for more cups, and we stood drinking coffee rather awkwardly until the second battalion commander turned up. I couldn't help being impressed by the speed with which the Army acted on the brigadier's orders. When we were assembled he gave the three officers a quick briefing. "You must consider yourselves on active service," he said. "I cannot explain now, but a situation has arisen in which the independence of Nueva is gravely threatened, and only swift action by the Army can preserve it. I am counting on your absolute loyalty to carry out orders even if you do not fully understand the reason for them. I am trusting you, and I hope you can trust me."

"That goes without saying, sir," the senior of the two battalion commanders said.

The brigadier then gave orders for the two battalions to proceed at once to Chacarima, to hold the road, and picket the roadside bush. He went on, "Colonel Blair is going with you. You are not in any way under his command, but he is a true friend of our Nuevan people and it is my wish that you should treat him with the utmost respect, and, if he thinks fit to offer advice, to act on it as far as you can. I hope to be able to join you soon after midday. Theophilus, I want you to accompany Colonel Blair, and consider yourself his personal aide. Now I must leave you to get on with things, for I have an urgent meeting of the Chiefs of Staff to attend."

The brigadier went off. The battalion commanders had a brief discussion, and then the elder of the two—Lieutenant-Colonel Garcia—turned to me. "We shall be ready to move in about half an hour," he said. "I will pick you up here, and you and Captain Theophilus can travel in my car. Will that suit you?"

"Admirably," I said. They saluted, and went out together.

"What is supposed to happen to me?" Ruth asked.

"The lady will be well looked after here," Captain Theophilus said.

"The lady is not going to be looked after here. I'm not going to be dumped. I haven't even got anything to read."

I didn't like the idea of Ruth's being mixed up in a military operation, but we'd been through so much together that I didn't want to abandon her. And she knew more about the earthquake process than anyone else on our side. "I think Mrs Caval had better come with us. I'll take full responsibility," I said. The young captain bowed politely.

I wanted to get rid of him. Ruth had no idea of what was happening, and I couldn't explain things with my attentive aide-de-camp hanging around. "Has anybody paid Elias?" I asked.

"I don't think he wants paying—he's very much concerned about Mr Caval, and only too anxious to help," Ruth said.

"He ought to be paid. I'm sure Caval would want it." I had a 100-dollar Nuevan note in my pocket book and I gave the note to Captain Theophilus. "Would you mind giving this to the driver who brought you back from the hospital?" I said. "He's a man called Elias—I don't know if he has any other names—and he runs a garage at Partika. He has rendered the Nuevan State considerable service this morning, and it's more than likely that your Government will want to acknowledge it in due course. So could you get personal particulars from him, and make a note of them? And he's not had so much as a cup of coffee since leaving Partika—it would be a kindly act if you could arrange something for him, and then tell him to go back home."

The captain gave an impeccable salute and went off to deal with Elias.

"Thank you for not deserting me," Ruth said.

"Don't be silly. There's a fearful lot to tell you, but that chap will be away only a few minutes, and I can't talk while he's here. Briefly, the Army's going out in force to try to forestall that meeting in the caves. It means deposing the Prime Minister, and an Army takeover of the Government. I don't know if it will work, but it's the only chance left in the time available. Anyway, Brigadier Ezra, who seems the most powerful personality in the Army, is game to try. He's gone off to a meeting of the Chiefs of Staff to set up a military junta. I hope he succeeds, but he himself is already committed—two battalions are on the move to Chacarima, and we're going with one of the battalion commanders."

"Quick work, Peter! I don't know how you did it, but it's very exciting."

"Luck, mostly, and that remark the Prime Minister made in the cave about not trusting the Army to support his bid for dictatorship. And having two such mates as you and old Caval."

"Poor Mr Caval. I'm afraid he's badly hurt, and I don't think we did him any good in moving him."

"He'd have died if he'd stayed on the cliff, or put an end to himself with his Mannlicher. We've given him a chance, and perhaps the Nuevan people a chance. What was it he said 'Three against the world!' Do you remember?"

She just squeezed my hand.

If Lieutenant-Colonel Garcia was surprised at having a woman added to his party, he accepted Ruth's presence philosophically. There was plenty of room in the big American staff car. Captain Theophilus sat in front with the Army driver, Ruth and I sat in the back with the colonel.

The Nuevan Army might be small, but it was well equipped, and when we came to the turning for the Chacarima road we met an apparently endless column of troop-carrying trucks. I thought we'd have a long wait to turn into the road, but the column was well controlled by military police on motor cycles, and as soon as the battalion commander's car was seen a motor cycle patrol halted the line of trucks to make a space for us to join it.

We didn't talk much on the journey. The battalion commander politely refrained from questioning me, and I didn't feel able to say anything about the object of the manoeuvres in the absence of the brigadier. I was glad when we came to the Chacarima

131

ridge and could get on with doing things. The deployment of the troops seemed to me practical and efficient. They had been ordered to hold the Chacarima road and to command the ridge —they had not yet been ordered to descend to the Chacarima Inlet. A little below the summit of the ridge a dirt-road from the bush met the metalled road. The dirt-road was a timber trail, and a short way along it was a wide clearing, where forest trees had been felled. The vehicles were drawn up here, and an advance party had set up a command post. The other battalion commander was already there. "There are pickets on both sides of the road," he said, "and I'm holding the main body of men here in the bush. Do you think we ought to send scouts down to the coast?"

"It would be a good idea," I said. "I doubt if they will find much to report, but you should command both banks of the Carima river, and it is possible that someone may come ashore from the caves. I can't give you instructions, but if anyone does come ashore my view is that he should be detained and brought to you."

"Fine," said Garcia, "we'll see to it at once. Now if you and the lady will go across to that covered truck you'll find our field Mess being set up, and it's more than time for breakfast."

Captain Theophilus escorted us, and in a couple of minutes I had a drink in my hands. I had barely started drinking it when there was a noise of a helicopter, and an Army machine came down in the clearing. The brigadier and a small group of other men in uniform climbed out of it. I walked over to meet him, and the first thing I noticed was that he was no longer a brigadier —he was wearing the insignia of a major-general.

"Congratulations," I said.

He was pleased that I'd noticed. "Everything went well," he said. "It's too long a story to go into now, but several of us have been unhappy about the Prime Minister for some time. As I expected, the Chief of Staff was reluctant that we should do anything, but he was in a minority of one. The rest of our Staff Council was convinced that we'd got to act. They decided to promote me to major-general, and appointed me as chairman of a military committee of three to form a provisional Government. You don't know my two colleagues, but they are excellent men, and old friends. They are staying in Fort James to announce the suspension of the constitution, and to put Nueva temporarily under military law. There will be no bloodshed. We are assured of the complete loyalty of the Army, and we shall hold elections for a new civilian Government as soon as we can. All Government officials have been told to stay at their posts, and to carry on as normally as possible. The diplomatic representatives have been informed. They are naturally shocked, but I think that there is nothing that they can do. I have said that I shall try to arrange a meeting with them tomorrow. Now I'd like to join you in a drink."

"And the Navy?" I asked.

"Well, we're doing what we can. As you suggested, our gunboat and a couple of escorting launches sailed some time ago. They should be in position off the Chacarima Inlet about now. As we came up we had a good view of the Inlet from the helicopter. There is no sign of any vessel, or of anything moving there. What do you think is our best approach to the caves?"

I had been thinking about this, and not much liking my thoughts. It was really a naval operation. The launches could land men at the mouth of the cave, and they could go in by the rough path that ran above sea-level. But it was a narrow path, and the defenders, if they chose to fight, were in a damnably strong position. We could send the launches into the caves, but they were not armoured, and could not carry many men. They would be vulnerable to rifle or even revolver fire, and we could not risk losing the launches, for we appeared to have only two of them. There was probably enough water for the gunboat to go in. She could take enough men to storm the place, but with the freighter already there room for manoeuvre was severely limited. If the gunboat were damaged there would be nothing left to intercept the yacht carrying the Chinese emissary.

"Do you know the caves at all?" I asked.

"No," he said. "Everybody in Nueva knows about the Chacarima caves, but Nuevan people do not go there very much. There is talk about making them a tourist attraction, and if this coast were developed for tourism, doubtless they would become one. As things are, the caves are scarcely visited at all."

I explained the general lie of the caves, as far as I had seen them. "The position," I went on, "is this. The Prime Minister and his party inside the caves cannot get out. You have complete command of the entrance, and as long as your gunboat remains in action her three-inch gun can deal with the freighter if she tries to make a dash for it. In time, you can certainly starve them out, but that may take a long time. I don't know what they've got in the way of stores, but they must have something because people have been living there, and the freighter herself may be well stocked with food. There is a route into the caves from the other side of the headland—the way Edward Caval took us in last night. But he knows it only because he explored the place as a boy. I think I could find it again, but it is not an easy route, and it would take time to assemble a force in any strength by using it. I doubt if anyone in the Prime Minister's party knows about it, but if they heard anything before you could have men there in strength, they could block it easily enough—a couple of men with rifles could hold the path against an Army.

"You may have to try to force the cave by the sea entrance. I'm sure you could do it, but it might be horribly costly in casualties. My own plan would be this. Mr Li Cook is expecting his Chinese visitor this afternoon. If your gunboat can intercept him, he won't arrive. The cave party won't know what is happening, and the chances are that somebody—maybe the Prime Minister himself—will come out before dark to have a look. I should rather expect it to be the Prime Minister—he can't risk staying away from Fort James for long. When is he supposed to be due back from Barbados?"

"Tomorrow morning."

"There you are—he'll almost certainly want to get out of the caves tonight."

Ruth was beside me throughout this conversation. "You can't be sure that he doesn't know what's happening," she said. "They talked about getting a radio message from the American yacht. If they've got radio, they may know about the Army take-over."

"They can't yet," Major-General Ezra said. "We discussed radio at our meeting. I was concerned not to frighten off our Chinese visitor—if he got news of a Nuevan *coup d'état* on his yacht, he'd just turn round and go off again. And although we can't hold him for long, we want to know who he is, and to make sure that he doesn't go home with any wrong ideas. So we decided to broadcast nothing over the radio today. We've occupied the Radio Nueva building, and the staff there have been ordered to carry on with completely normal programmes."

"News might get out through Press representatives in Fort James, or by diplomatic channels," I said. "It doesn't matter where it's broadcast from—if it goes on the air at all, we must assume they'll know about it."

"Well, news can only get out quickly by telephone or cable. I agree that we can't keep things secret for more than a few hours, but we need only a few hours. I told you that we have a good Army Signals section. They've arranged a technical hitch in the Nuevan telephone service—there isn't really a hitch, of course, but anyone who tries to put through an international call won't be able to. We have also occupied the cable building, and imposed a censorship on messages. I know we're not supposed to hold up diplomatic messages, but some delay will, I fear, occur."

"You have certainly earned your promotion," I said.

X

CAT AND MOUSE

I WAS IMPRESSED by the Nuevan Army Staff's fore-thought about radio, but radio silence was also a nuisance, because it meant that we couldn't communicate with the gunboat. Ezra had given instructions for the two launches to come in to the beach, and after our Nuevan breakfast (otherwise an early lunch) I went down to the inlet with Lieutenant-Colonel Strong, who had been appointed liaison officer with the naval force. We got there a little ahead of the boats, but we could see them coming in and they anchored a few minutes later. The officer in charge, a young lieutenant, came ashore in a rubber dinghy.

The gunboat, he told us, was on station about half a mile east of the high ground enclosing the eastern side of the Chacarima Inlet, which meant that she couldn't be seen from the inlet itself. Her commander had been told to await orders.

"I think we'd better go out to her," I said to Strong. "We can't use R/T and there's too much to explain for written orders. She can't be more than about three miles away, and we should be on board in a quarter of an hour or so. I suggest that we go out in one of the launches, while the other waits here. Tell them to be armed and ready for action, and to arrest anyone who may come out from the Chacarima caves."

Strong agreed to this. The lieutenant decided to stay with the waiting launch, and we went out in the other. They were good boats, about forty feet long, armed with heavy machine guns fore and aft, and carrying a crew of twelve. The officer in command of our launch told us that she could do nearly thirty knots and was a fine seaboat, having been built originally for the U.S. Coastguard Service. We soon raised the gunboat, still bearing her old Royal Navy name *Penelope*, but now N.N.S. (Nuevan Naval Ship) instead of H.M.S. Her commander was an elderly captain, who had served in the British Merchant Marine, and in the RNVR. He received us formally at the top of *Penelope's* boarding ladder, with a smart guard drawn up to meet us, and a piper to pipe us on board.

"I'm thankful to see you," he said. "We left in a great hurry this morning with orders to patrol here, but I've very little idea what we're supposed to do. I hope you've brought some instructions for me."

"We have," replied Strong. "Can we go to your cabin?"

Strong introduced me. "Colonel Blair is a British officer who is acting as a military adviser to our Nuevan Army commander, Major-General Ezra. I take it that you do not know of the events in Fort James this morning?"

"I know nothing. I received orders to put to sea at once, and did so."

"Much has happened since then," Strong said. "Our Army Intelligence Service discovered a plot against the independence of Nueva, an exceedingly grave business in which, I am sorry to say, the former Prime Minister, Mr Li Cook, is deeply implicated. The Army had to act at once. The Army Council has temporarily suspended the Nuevan constitution, put Nueva under military law, deposed Mr Li Cook, and appointed a Provisional Military Government, under Major-General Ezra, to govern Nueva until arrangements can be made for new elections. I have formally to ask you whether you are prepared to serve our Military Government."

The captain took off his cap and rubbed his nearly bald head. "Only a year to go before my pension," he said ruefully. "Obey orders if you break owners—that's an old Merchant Service saying. I had orders to come here, and I'm obeying them. When you give me more orders, I'll obey those, too. It's not for me to say who runs the Government. I know about your man Ezra, though I thought he was a brigadier, and I've a lot of respect for him. O.K. man. Tell me what I've got to do."

Strong turned to me. "It might be helpful if Colonel Blair explained some things in a bit more detail."

"Gladly," I said. "It is not for me to go into the plot against Nueva. It has nothing to do with my Government—except that we are friends of Nueva, and want to help if we can. A new military weapon, of, perhaps, considerable importance, has been secretly developed in the Chacarima caves. We obtained information that Mr Li Cook was prepared to sell this secret to the

Chinese, in return for an alliance with the Chinese to establish himself as dictator of Nueva backed by sufficient Chinese force to destroy the Nuevan Army and keep him in power. The Nuevan Army's reaction to this you have heard. A Chinese envoy is on his way to settle things in a chartered American yacht. She is due off Chacarima this afternoon. Lieutenant-Colonel Strong will, I think, confirm that the new Nuevan Government wishes you to intercept this yacht, put a naval party on board to detain her radio operator, and prevent any use of radio, and escort her to Fort James, where a military guard will be waiting to take over from you."

"That is correct," said Strong. I think it was probably the first he had heard of most of the things I mentioned, but he supported me loyally.

"Some job," said the captain. "What if she resists?"

"The vessel is a yacht, and is unlikely to have anything in the way of armament," I said. "Your three-inch gun should give you complete superiority. It is possible that there may be people on board armed with rifles or revolvers, and that they will try to resist arrest. If so, you must meet force with force, and, if necessary, use your gun. You are well within Nuevan territorial waters, and if she tries to resist arrest you are entitled to use superior force on the orders of your Government."

"Well, I'll get the gun manned and some shells up, though we haven't had much gunnery practice. What time do you expect this yacht to turn up, and what is her name?"

"We don't know her name. We do know that she is described as a big yacht, and that she is due this afternoon. My own guess is that you can expect her any time now. She must be here well before dark, in time for the people on board to attend a demonstration which requires daylight."

The captain went off to see about the gun. "Do you think we ought to stay?" Strong asked. "I'm sure the old chap will do his best, but I can't say that I feel a great deal of confidence in him."

"You've a damned good little Army, but you don't seem to have taken your Navy all that seriously," I said.

"We haven't had much time. There was local recruitment to the Nuevan Regiment in British days, which gives us something of an Army tradition. At sea everything was in the hands of the Royal Navy. It's left a gap which we haven't filled."

"Well, that's for the future. As of now, I'd like to get back to Major-General Ezra, but I'm afraid I agree with you—I think we ought to stay on board. The old man is probably a good seaman, but he may need stiffening when it comes to dealing with matters far outside his own experience. We can stay for a bit, anyway."

As things turned out, we didn't have to wait long, for the captain came back a few minutes later to say, "There's a ship on the horizon now, which may be the yacht you were speaking of. Would you like to get the glasses on her?"

The ship was already visible to the naked eye, and through a pair of good naval binoculars she came up sharply. Yes, she could certainly be a big steam, or more probably diesel, yacht. She had yacht lines, and she was moving fast. Soon I could identify her ensign—it was clearly a U.S. flag.

"Undoubtedly looks like her, and she seems to be on course for the Chacarima Inlet," I said. "We'd better steam towards her, and be ready to order her to stop. It may be necessary to send a round across her bow—you can aim well ahead of her to make sure of not hitting her by accident. But don't fire yet. We must get a closer look at her. Have the gun ready, though."

Then the yacht blew up.

It was a devastating explosion—one moment she was there, a fine-looking vessel of some 600–800 tons standing in towards the Chacarima Inlet, the next she was a mass of debris, almost disintegrated. The gunboat's captain needed no telling what to do—distress at sea was something he understood instinctively. We were already steaming towards the wreck, now not more than a couple of miles away. He ordered the lifeboats to be swung out, and the sickbay got ready to receive injured survivors.

I kept my glasses on the wreckage, though there was little left to see above the water. My mind was racing. What had Charles Caval said in the cave? "We have arranged a demonstration for him. . . . It will have to be at sea, of course. . . ." Could something have gone wrong? Could that diabolical machinery have brought about a marine earthquake too soon?

But that was no earthquake, it was an explosion. The sea remained relatively calm, and we had felt nothing on the gunboat. Either there had been some violent explosion on board, or she had struck an exceptionally powerful mine. A mine! My God, could that have been an insurance policy for Charles's demonstration? A mine could be set off by radio. But if there had been a radio controlled mine, would it have gone off on being struck? Well, it had gone off—the "how" didn't matter at the moment. Charles had spoken of a demonstration over a defined area—if there had been one mine, could there be others?

We were closing the wreckage rapidly. I called urgently to the captain, "Bear away and stop her. On no account go the other side of the wreck. Get boats lowered as soon as you can to investigate, but don't take your ship any nearer than she is now."

The launch had also made for the wreckage, and was almost up to it. "Radio," I said. "It doesn't matter now! I *must* speak to the launch."

There was a naval walkie-talkie outfit on the bridge. The captain gave it to me and I called urgently *"Penelope* to launch, *Penelope* to launch. I have an important message for you."

Discipline on that launch was good, for although they had not been using radio their radio set was manned. "Launch to *Penelope*. Reading you loud and clear. Proceed with message. Over." Thankfully I heard the response. I told them to reduce speed, make what search they could for survivors, and not to go beyond the wreck. "Keep a sharp look-out for mines," I added.

By the time I had finished speaking the boats were being lowered. I borrowed the captain's loud-hailer and repeated the warning about mines.

There were no survivors. Two bodies were picked up dead, and brought on board the gunboat. One was Chinese, the other European. As the European body was laid out on the deck, the captain said, "I know that man! He has sailed with me often when I worked on the inter-island packet boats. It is Mr Nicolas Caval."

No one had seen anything that looked like a mine, but neither the launch nor the lifeboats had searched in the area where I thought it most likely that mines would be, if there were any to

140

be found. I marked it on the captain's chart. "Until it can be swept it must be regarded as a danger area," I said.

I asked Lieutenant-Colonel Strong to order the gunboat to enter the Chacarima Inlet and to anchor about half a mile off the entrance to the caves. "Tell him to keep steam up, and to be ready to slip his cable and give chase at a moment's notice," I said. "It would also be a good idea to get his gun trained on the cave entrance. He should get his searchlight ready, too."

We didn't wait to return to the inlet with the gunboat. The launch which had been searching the wreckage was called alongside, we went on board, and she took us back to the beach at speed.

There had been a considerable build-up of troops while we were away. A whole company was now installed at the western end of the beach, within rifle-range of the entrance to the caves. Another company was in reserve at the eastern end. I suggested to Strong that when the gunboat arrived at least half of the men in the reserve company should be ferried out to her launches—they would add substantially to the gunboat's firepower if it became necessary to force the entrance.

The men on the beach had seen the explosion out to sea, and were anxious to know what it was. Since radio was still not being used a dispatch rider had been sent to Major-General Ezra with news of the explosion, though obviously he could give no details. This man had just returned, with a message from Ezra asking that I should go to him at the command post on the ridge as soon as I could be got ashore. The launch that had remained by the beach was about to go out to recover me from the gunboat when the other launch brought us back.

Strong, as liaison officer with the naval branch of the Nuevan armed forces, felt that he had better stay on the beach. I went back to the ridge in a jeep. It was a rough ride over parts of the unmade track, but men were at work clearing undergrowth and filling the worst ruts with an amalgam of twigs, small branches and earth, making the track much more usable for vehicles.

Ezra was relieved to see me. So was Ruth. She had been valuable to him in being able to describe the installations in the cave and he did his best to be nice to her, but he was frantically busy in dealing with messages from Fort James as well as organising the military side of the operation, and for much of the time Ruth had been on her own, not knowing what was happening and increasingly worried about me.

I gave a rapid account of the explosion and of what seemed to me the puzzling features of it. "I do not believe that it was any sort of earthquake," I said. "There was no tidal wave, nothing to indicate any disturbance on the seabed. It was undoubtedly a very severe explosion. Of course it could have been an explosion on the yacht, but if so it was an extraordinary coincidence that it should happen where it did. My own guess is that the sea area was mined, to provide an explosion where it was wanted if the earthquake system didn't work."

"That would be like Charles," Ruth said. "He had negotiated his big deal, and he wouldn't care a cent if part of it was faked."

"I think we can leave that for the moment," I said. "What matters is that the ship and the Chinese envoy are gone. The fact that a Chinese body was picked up virtually proves that the ship was carrying the Chinese envoy—if you are expecting a ship with Chinese on board to appear at a given time and place, and such a ship does appear, it's stretching coincidence too far to bother about the possibilty that it was a quite different ship, with quite different Chinese. We don't know if the body was that of the envoy, or of a member of his staff—maybe we shall never know. We can assume that the ship was the envoy's ship, and that the envoy is now dead."

"Yes, we can assume that," Ezra said.

"It changes the whole situation," I went on. "Before the explosion there was always a risk that the cave party was in radio contact with the ship—in fact, we know they were—and that they might send a signal warning off the ship, or asking the ship to create a diversion or bring help from somewhere. They can't do that any longer. I think it's time to use radio in a big way. Get Fort James to broadcast news of the overthrow of the Prime Minister and the setting up of military government. The broadcast is almost bound to be picked up in the cave. Allow a little time for it to sink in, and then try to establish radio contact with the cave. Tell them their position is hopeless and that their only chance is to give themselves up."

Ezra considered this for a moment. Then he said, "I think you are right. Having agreed not to use radio I'm a bit doubtful of going on the air to Fort James—they may suspect that things have gone wrong in some way. But I've kept the helicopter—that can get back to Fort James quickly, and I'll send a written message with an officer who will be trusted. What about young Theophilus? He is my own aide. Do you need him any longer?"

"He has been most helpful, and I wouldn't like him to think that we just don't want him. But we certainly don't need him."

"I'll see that his feelings aren't hurt. Right, I'll get things moving."

When he'd gone, I asked Ruth, "What do you make of the other body's being Nicolas Caval?"

"Charles's father? Oh God, Peter, I don't know."

"Obviously he was very much mixed up in things. Presumably he was the main contact with Li Cook, and it looks as though he was the go-between with the Chinese. It may sound mad, but I can't help feeling that the main impulse on the Nicolas-Charles side came from that old family feud with the Edward Cavals. They appear to have hated our Edward, and they have always wanted his money and his land. It's fairly clear now that they tried to kill him at Chacarima. As their share, or part of their share, in the deal with Li Cook they may have demanded that Edward Caval should be disposed of and his property transferred to them. As dictator of Nueva Li Cook would have been able to do that."

Ruth shuddered.

We heard the helicopter take off and Ezra walked back to us. "The helicopter won't take more than twenty minutes to get to Fort James, and we should be on the air in half an hour or so," he said. "Now I must get hold of our signals officer. He'll be delighted to have something to do. It must be tiresome to have all that lovely equipment and be ordered to keep radio silence."

The mobile signals' unit was housed in a couple of vans, under the command of an alert and clearly well trained captain. His first job was to prepare for the reception of the broadcast from Fort James, which simply meant tuning in to the station. Ezra's timing was almost exactly right—in thirty-one minutes from the departure of the helicopter we heard the announcer saying "Stand by for an important announcement." Then came the Nuevan national anthem, and a statement declaring, "This is an official announcement by the new Government of Nueva. A most grave crisis threatening the independence of our State has been averted by the Army. It has been necessary to remove Mr Li Cook from the post of Prime Minister and temporarily to suspend the constitution. The Army Council has appointed a committee of three, under Major-General Ezra, to form the provisional military government of Nueva. No one who has not taken part in the plot against the State has anything to fear. All Government officials, police and schoolteachers have been ordered to remain in their posts and to carry on exactly as before. All business men and private citizens are asked to carry on with their normal work in the normal way. As soon as possible the provisional military government will organise the holding of elections to provide civilian government again. Long live Nueva."

The signals' captain's next job was to try to establish radio contact with the cave. "Have you any idea what sort of equipment they have?" he asked.

"No, but there is a deep-water anchorage in the cave and a fair-sized modern freighter is almost certainly still there," I said. "She will have the usual marine radio installation. I should try calling on the standard marine frequency and see what happens."

"Do you know the freighter's name?"

"No, because when I saw her it appeared to have been painted out. Try calling 'Chacarima caves'."

The captain operated the set himself. "Nuevan Army calling Chacarima caves," he said. He repeated the call twice. Then, "Can you read me? Over."

Ezra, a small group of officers with him, Ruth and I waited in tense silence. The captain had the handset, and the rest of us could do nothing but watch his face. Nothing happened. He called again, and again there was no response. "Doesn't seem to raise anyone," he said. "We're on high ground and the distance is not great. We ought to be able to get through. Of course, their radio may not be manned, or possibly there is radio obstruction in the formation of the caves."

"There may be, but from the way they spoke when I overheard them I certainly formed the impression that they had received a radio message in the cave."

"Try again," Ezra said.

There was still no response.

"They may be reading you all right and just staying off the air themselves," I said. "How about giving them a bit more information? Something like, 'If you have not already done so, tune in to Fort James radio. Your plot has been discovered. The Nuevan Army is in force at Chacarima, and a gunboat is patrolling the inlet. You cannot escape. Your only chance is to give yourselves up. You will have a fair trial. If you try to stay where you are you have no chance at all'."

"Sounds all right—can you write it down, Colonel?" Ezra said. "We can try it, anyway."

I wrote my suggested message on a signal pad and gave it to the captain. He called again, and read it out. I thought that we had met the usual blank response, when suddenly his whole being seemed to leap into activity. He seized a pad and wrote furiously. Then he spoke into the set again, "Message received. Stand by for further communication." He gave the signal pad to Ezra, who read the message to us. It was arrogant and defiant.

"You are fools," it ran. "This is an ultimatum. It is now four o'clock. Unless Brigadier Ezra—I do not like usurped rank —comes alone into the cave, unarmed and carrying a white flag, before five o'clock, the Chacarima ridge and all the men on it will be destroyed. Ordered by the Prime Minister of Nueva."

"Get them again," Ezra said, "and give the phone to me." The captain called as before, and added, "I am now giving the handset to Major-General Ezra. Stand by for him."

Ezra said, "This is Major-General Ezra. I assume I am speaking to Mr Li Cook. Your attitude is futile. We are Nuevan soldiers, and all Nuevan soldiers are ready to give their lives for Nueva. If by some diabolical means you contrive to kill some of us our comrades will storm your cave and they will not be inclined to show you any mercy. And if you kill all of us here, there are many more brave Nuevan soldiers to take our places. You and those with you must come out, in your ship if you like, and give yourselves up. A naval gun is trained on the entrance to the cave. If you try to run for it, your ship will be sunk. I promise you a fair trial—nothing more. If you do not accept this offer I shall order the cave to be stormed. I give you until four-thirty. I repeat, four-thirty. Over."

We could hear the faint sounds of a live telephone coming

from the R/T receiver, but could not make out any words. When Ezra put down the handset his face was grave. "He threatens to destroy the whole of Fort James," he said.

Asking Lieutenant-Colonel Garcia to stay with him Ezra sent the other officers to their posts. He told the signals' captain to maintain a constant radio watch on the cave, to send any messages to him at once, but not to engage in any conversation other than that required for signals procedure. Then he beckoned to Ruth and me, and the four of us walked to a little glade about a hundred yards away, where we were alone.

"I am wondering if it is not my duty to surrender. The destruction he threatens to civilians is too terrible to contemplate," he said.

"It is one thing to threaten, it is quite another to perform," I remarked, though I was not feeling the confidence I tried to show.

"Something destroyed Chacarima House."

"Whatever that something was it did not destroy the American yacht."

"How can you be sure of that?"

"For two reasons. First, the physical appearance of the explosion—it was definitely an explosion, and not an earthquake. My second reason is more a matter of inference, but I think it is quite valid. If you assume that the explosion at sea was brought about by some action from the cave, why did it happen when it did? He needed the safe arrival of the yacht—he could have no conceivable purpose in destroying her."

"A mistake while experimenting?"

"Possibly. But there remains the physical evidence of the sort of explosion it was. I think it probable that there are at least one, perhaps two, other mines. That could be checked by sweeping the area."

"There is not time."

"I respect your feelings, Major-General, but surely there is another important consideration," Garcia said. "If you surrender, Mr Li Cook will simply return to power. Can we accept as the ruler of Nueva a man who is prepared to destroy Fort James, with the appalling loss and suffering that would bring, for his own purposes?"

Ezra looked at his watch: it was seventeen minutes past four.

"My ultimatum expires in thirteen minutes," he said. "If I am not going to give in I should order an attack on the cave."

"There's someone coming from the signals truck," Ruth said. A runner came up, and our spirits rose a little. Had the cave party decided to give in?

Ezra read out the signal. "If you attempt to storm the cave I shall act at once. If there is no attack I am prepared to wait until five o'clock. If by that time Brigadier Ezra has not presented himself alone as instructed Fort James will be devastated. By order. The Prime Minister."

The runner was waiting. "There is no reply," Ezra said.

It was twenty-two minutes past four.

If Ezra's nerve had been shaken, he had recovered it. I admired the man tremendously. "I shall call up Strong on the beach and order the troops to go in at half-past four," he said.

"Don't," I said. "Keep him guessing. He's all ready to meet an assault, and he may have considerable small-arms fire. If the troops go in at half-past four there will be heavy casualities."

"If they don't go in, Fort James may be destroyed."

Ruth broke in, "Can you get me a map? It ought to be a geological map, but if there isn't one can I have any map of the area?"

"I can get you a map after I've called up Lieutenant-Colonel Strong."

"Please—please. Don't let any men be killed until I have seen the map. I've been thinking desperately, and I may be able to tell you why the Chacarima earthquake worked, and why I don't think any others will."

"She knows more about this than anybody else. Hold up your order and let her see the map," I said.

"All right, but only for a few minutes." Garcia ran to the signals truck and came back with a big map-case. "These are the old surveys of our colonial days, that's why they are in inches," he said. "There is an inch-to-the-mile sheet similar to the old British Ordnance Survey maps but, I fear, less accurate, and a $2\frac{1}{2}$ inches-to-the-mile sheet which is better because it has some up-to-date revisions for the benefit of the tourist industry. It covers a much smaller area, of course."

"I'll have the larger-scale map. It will have to do."

Ruth moved away a little, sat on the ground, and pored over the sheet. "I can only go roughly from the contours and the pattern of vegetation, but I think I've got it," she said. "From the caves to the site of the old Chacarima House seems just the shape of earth formation that Phil used as a model for his work. It is fundamentally unstable—there've been earthquake shocks at Chacarima before. And the distance from the caves is short— that's why the maths and Phil's radio-wave shock principle could work. I can't tell anything about the seabed, but looking at the shape of the land on that side of the Chacarima Inlet, it's quite different from the land round Chacarima House. It's a much more stable formation, and I don't believe that Phil's process could work in that area. I suspect that Charles tried it after he'd killed Phil, found he couldn't get anywhere, and used mines instead. He'd probably been thinking of ordinary high-explosive as an insurance policy all along, and I daresay the freighter brought a good supply.

"This sheet goes nowhere near Fort James, but it covers a bit of this ridge. Everything this side of the Carima River looks quite stable, and I don't believe they could do anything to affect the ridge, still less to touch anything beyond it as far away as Fort James."

Ezra looked undecided. He turned to me, "You suggest we simply call his bluff?"

"Yes. Let him wait till five o'clock. Let him start up all his bloody machines. If nothing happens, he'll know that he hasn't any power left."

"It's an appalling gamble."

"It's not quite a gamble. I am a mathematician, and I know something about the process," Ruth said.

It was twenty-three minutes to five. A little wind rustled the leaves of the forest-covered ridge. The clearing, for all the Army vehicles parked round it, looked extraordinarily peaceful. Ezra was wrestling not only with his problem, but with himself. Ignorant as most of us are about mathematics, in the European and American world we have been battered by the Einsteins and the atom splitters into some kind of submission to the physicists and mathematicians. Ezra's people were of older human stock, atavistic fears of magic nearer to the surface of their mind. He himself had probably no Carib blood, but the ancient Carib ways of thought permeated the subconscious minds of many of his people. The Chacarima caves were the abode of strange powers, the preserve of the jealous spirit of the Carima River. The power to bring about earthquakes was magic, dangerous, devilish magic, but not necessarily unreal—indeed, the very fear of it made it seem the more likely that in some horrible way it might be real. A cool mathematical judgment might influence Ezra's reason; it had much less influence on his subconscious imagination.

Reason won. It was nineteen minutes to five.

"Should we send a signal to Fort James to warn people just in case anything happens?" Ezra asked.

"No," I said. "Such a signal could only cause panic. You've decided on a course of action, and if the reasons for the decision are good there's no need to send a signal."

"It's damned hard to wait."

"Think of the people waiting in the cave. Their nerve must be near cracking. Li Cook can't exactly want to destroy Fort James, even if he thinks he can. It won't exactly make him popular."

"We can't see anything from here," Ruth said. "Do you think we could go back to the road? A little way along, where it crosses the summit, we can see over the inlet."

It was a valuable interruption. "Sure," said Ezra. "We'll go in my car."

He didn't send for a driver but took the wheel himself. I got in beside him, Ruth and Garcia in the back. The earth track had been much churned up by vehicles and the car needed careful handling. By the time we had negotiated the track back to the road, and driven along the road to the summit, it was six minutes to five.

The road crossed the summit through a cutting. The inshore bank was wooded, the bank on the coastal side of the road here was a great slab of exposed rock. We got out of the car and climbed the rock. From the top there was a superb view over the inlet. We could see the huge archway that was the entrance to the Chacarima caves, the gunboat, looking like a toy boat, anchored in the bay. My watch had a sweep second-hand, and this was the hand to look at now. There was only seconds to go.

"He'll be pulling his switches now," I said. "Ruth seems to have been right."

But was she? Even as the words left my lips we were conscious of a low, sickening rumble. The rock on which we stood remained quite firm, the trees on the ridge moved gently in the breeze. But something was happening to the massive headland that towered over the Chacarima caves. Rocks were tumbling down the sheer cliffs, the whole central mass of the headland seemed to be caving in. The low rumble changed to a tremendous roar and a huge plume of white water soared into the sky. It was as if the great waterfall inside the caves had suddenly been reversed, to be hurled upwards instead of cascading into its ravine. We must have been a good three miles away, but we were drenched with spray from it. Like heavy rain, the spray blotted out all vision.

"My God, the reciprocal effect!" Ruth said. "I told you it could sometimes happen. They've brought the whole headland tumbling down on themselves!"

The spray lasted only for a minute or so. When it cleared we could see what appeared to be an enormous crater where the top of the headland had been. The archway making the sea entrance to the caves was shattered, and the channel was now open to the sky. There were some heavy waves breaking on the beach, but the gunboat was still there, and there didn't seem to be any particular damage to the foreshore.

"Nothing more can happen now," Ruth said. "The whole of that cave system must have been unstable, and a reciprocal shock wave, coming back from the stable structure of the ridge, sent it crashing. I wonder why there wasn't a tidal wave in the inlet?"

"The cave system we used from the other side of the headland may have acted as a safety valve," I said. "There may be tremendous damage in that other bay. As nobody seems to live there perhaps it doesn't matter much."

XI

BACK TO LONDON

W E DIDN'T GET back to Fort James until nearly ten o'clock, and Major-General Ezra invited Ruth and me to stay at his house. The alternative was the hotel, and we were both too tired to want to deal with any more people, even hotel receptionists.

Ezra ordered a meal for us, but couldn't stay to eat with us, for he had to rush off to a meeting of the Provisional Government. He did find time to have a drink with us beforehand.

"I can't hope to thank either of you adequately," he said. "You will be heroes in our history books."

"If I'm still your military adviser I'd like to offer a bit more advice," I told him. "You will have to produce a very much edited story for public consumption. So far only you and a few of your Staff officers know anything about what was really going on in those caves. The late Prime Minister is known to have been there. You can say that the caves contained a powerful build-up of weapons for the purpose of overthrowing the Nuevan State, and that Li Cook had gone there to meet agents for the recruitment of foreign mercenaries to establish him in power. By good Army intelligence you got wind of this, cornered Li Cook in the caves, and forestalled the landing of any foreign troops. The explosion is best left suitably vague. The caves were full of arms and explosives, and something can easily have gone off. The local Caribs won't believe a word of this. They'll put it down to the just anger of the Carima River, and in a way that's a tenable point of view. Let it pass into folklore. You don't have to say anything about it yourself; it will come about naturally, and it will do you no harm if people feel that Nueva's great river came to the rescue of the Nuevan people at a critical moment. The less said about Ruth and me the better. Praise old Edward Caval —he's a Chacarima man, he's almost a Nuevan legend himself, and it's entirely fitting that he should have got wind of what was happening in his caves, and warned you. Give a few hints of this to your Press and radio journalists, and leave them to it. That should take care of your home front.

"On the diplomatic front you're going to have trouble, but with any luck you can turn the situation to Nueva's advantage. You can't ignore what you know about the caves, and while I myself doubt if artificial earthquakes have any future the mere rumour of someone's possessing the power to create them is enough to upset the world. If you play your cards properly it will turn out that you've done civilisation a very good turn. If you continue to trust me, I can probably help you here. I can see that the right people in England and America know all about it, and what a horrible conspiracy was nipped in the bud by your prompt action. I'd suggest that you invite a combined British-American Scientific Mission to come to Nueva for some quite general purpose—say to investigate the possibilities of getting large-scale hydro-electric power from the Chacarima region. In reality they can investigate what's left of the caves, and work out whether there is anything at all in the artificial earthquake process. You can't do this yourselves. Somebody's going to do it, and if you get off to a good British-American start, perhaps bringing in the French and Germans too, you'll have a key place in the diplomatic scheme of things. But you must move quickly, and very quietly. Shout about Nuevan patriotism and the saving of Nueva—you've got a good deal to shout about—but keep artificial earthquakes under your hat."

He didn't reply directly. "There used to be a saying in this part of the world, 'Word of an Englishman'—you used it when you wanted to stress that a promise was going to be kept," he said. "Perhaps there was something in it. Now I really must go."

Ezra had a good cook and she'd turned out a nice meal for us—some kind of local fish, served with sweet potato and lightly toasted cassava bread. But neither of us was in the least hungry. We tried to eat for politeness's sake, but we felt a devastating sense of after-climax, of complete emotional exhaustion.

"I wish we were back on our old boat," Ruth said

"So do I. Why not? We can hire a car to take us to Partika, and I expect the dinghy's still there. Do you realise that it was only this morning that we left it? There's nothing to keep us here tonight. Let's go."

"Oh Peter, if only we could! But after that lecture you gave the Major-General! He may come back in the small hours and want to know this, that and the other. God knows what's going to happen tomorrow. I haven't got any clothes—being with you always seems to leave me without any clothes! I can't undress properly, and I don't know if I can go to sleep, but at least I've got a room where I can try. The best thing is for us both to see if we can get some sleep." She got up from the table and kissed me.

After she'd gone I helped myself to another glass of Ezra's rum, but I drank only half of it. Somehow I didn't even want a drink. I'd had only a few cat-nap's of sleep since leaving the Oyster Rocks, and more than anything else I needed sleep, though like Ruth I wasn't at all sure if I could go to sleep. Ruth was right, though, the best thing to do was to try.

I had no pyjamas either, and apart from taking off my shoes, I didn't bother to undress. I was wrong about not being able to go to sleep, for I think I must have dropped off as soon as I lay down on the bed. I was dragged back from an exquisite oblivion of sleep by somebody shaking my shoulder.

I woke reluctantly, but I must have had the best part of five hours' sleep for it was four a.m. There were two men in my room, Ezra and another man. Ezra was the man who was shaking my shoulder.

"I'm sorry to disturb you, Colonel, but there is news that is both sad and important. This is Mr Gomez Santorini, the leading lawyer in Fort James. He will explain."

Not having to dress, I just sat on the bed. Mr Santorini spoke in a precise lawyer's voice. "With great regret I have to inform you that Mr Edward Caval died in hospital about an hour ago," he said. "His condition deteriorated, it was decided that there must be an immediate operation, and he did not survive the operation.

"I have further to inform you that shortly after his admission to hospital yesterday Mr Caval sent for me and instructed me to draw up a will. I acted on his instructions, and the will was duly signed and witnessed yesterday afternoon. It is a short, concise document. After legacies of six months' pay to everyone in his employ, and making provision for the payment of pensions for life to all his personal servants, Mr Caval has left all the rest of his estate in equal shares to you and a Mrs Ruth Caval. What is more immediately important, he has appointed you his sole executors. It is a very large estate, and there are many necessary decisions to be taken. That is why I have felt it my duty to come to you at once. Major-General Ezra tells me that Mrs Ruth Caval is also staying here."

"As far as I know she is asleep," I said. "She is dog-tired and I don't think we need disturb her yet. What do you want me to do?" I found it hard to take in what he was saying.

Ezra helped with one rather sombre bit of information. "In the tropics," he said, "it is customary—indeed, it is proper—to hold funerals quickly. I should like to arrange a State funeral for Mr Caval this afternoon, and it is for the executors to approve this, and to decide where he is to be buried."

"There is a small Anglican church near the factory at Chacarima," said Mr Santorini. "It is served by one of the canons at Fort James cathedral. In the churchyard at Chacarima many of Mr Caval's forbears are buried. If I may make a suggestion it would seem fitting for Mr Caval to be interred there. If you approve, I will get in touch with the priest concerned and arrange for the interment after the State service in the cathedral."

"I shall be most grateful if you will—I'm sure Ruth would agree. What are the other matters?"

"There are many matters of a business nature—Mr Caval had large interests throughout Nueva, as well as substantial investments abroad. I have long looked after the legal side of his affairs, and his agent in Fort James has seen to the day-to-day running of his business concerns. I should explain that the Caval Estate Office is a considerable business in itself, employing some fifty people. It is necessary for the agent and myself to know if you and Mrs Ruth Caval wish us to continue. We shall, of course, be happy to do so, but we need the authority of the executors."

I told him that as far as I was concerned I should be only too thankful for him to go ahead, and that I hadn't the least doubt about Ruth's agreement. The lawyer gave a little bow. "That is a most generous expression of confidence," he said. "I shall prepare a short letter of instructions for myself and the agent, and bring it to you later in the morning for you and Mrs Ruth Caval to sign. I need trouble you no more for the present. May I repeat my sincere condolences in the sad death of Mr Edward Caval, and ask you to convey them to Mrs Ruth Caval when it is convenient for her to be disturbed?"

I assured him that all should be done as he wished, and Ezra took him away. He came back in about five minutes with a jug of marvellously smelling coffee.

"Well, I've had quite an eventful night, but you can read all about it in the papers," he said. "Things have gone extremely well. Li Cook was feared and not greatly liked, and people have been rushing to Government House all night to swear allegiance to the Provisional Government. We seem to be extraordinarily popular. I think perhaps we have opened a new and happier chapter of Nuevan history. On the matters you talked about last night—I think you will approve of our policy. I'll discuss this later, and I'd like you to meet my colleagues in the Provisional Government. You will find them intelligent, and very well disposed to you.

"Now may I congratulate you on becoming, in a propertied sense, at any rate, our leading citizen?"

"With Ruth," I said.

"With your Ruth, of course. I think it is wonderfully appropriate."

"You can always nationalise the lot."

"I suppose so. But I think it unlikely, Nueva owes you a considerable debt, you know."

"Political debts don't count for much."

"Political debts ... well, maybe ... it's a harsh world. But personal debts are another matter. And ours, Colonel, has been a very personal relationship."

*   *   *

"What are you going to do, Peter?" asked Sir Edmund Pusey.

"I don't know. When you sent me to Nueva you said that you were sending me on holiday. It didn't turn out quite like that."

"No. ... There must be relatively few people who return from a holiday in the Caribbean with vastly more money than they started with. How much is it, Peter?"

"Again I don't know. The accountants and the lawyers are still working on it, and as far as I can see most of them will have a job to their retirement. It's an awful lot of money. The Nuevan estates and businesses, in so far as they can be valued, are worth several millions, and investments in Britain, the United States, and Switzerland come to several millions more." My mind went back to that morning, now some six months ago, when I'd told Ruth of our startling joint inheritance. Poor Ruth. The thinking of a lifetime of pinching and scraping her way through college, of rebuilding her life after the collapse of her marriage, was too much for her to take it in. I'd suggested that she should come to England for a bit—she had never been in England. "Oh Peter," she said, "that would be lovely! But I don't see how I could possibly afford it. I've got to buy another lot of clothes, I've got to get back to my job...." It took a little time to assure her that the Caval Estate, now half hers, could probably finance a trip to England, *and* a new wardrobe.

We had flown to England two days later. Partly this was enforced by the need for me to get back to report to Pusey, partly I felt it imperative to get Ruth into wholly new surroundings. I'd had long sessions with Ezra and his colleagues before we left. They accepted my suggestions, and although I had no official status were content to leave things to my judgment. These discussions took up most of the time, but there were two things I managed to do. I couldn't leave our old *Duchess* stranded at Partika—the roadstead in which she was anchored would not be safe in all weathers, and she was important to the economy of Naurataka. So I sent a car to collect her skipper and a crew from Naurataka, to sail her home. And Ezra and I fitted in a trip by helicopter over the Chacarima Inlet.

The inlet itself seemed virtually unchanged, but the headland over the caves, and the bay where we had anchored our old *Duchess* were transformed. The caves were gone, having become a steep-sided fjord, making a new mouth for the Carima River. My guess that the secondary cave-system by which we had entered for our night journey underground had acted as a sort of safety valve in the chaos of destruction had been more or less right. There was now an impressive waterfall cascading down the cliff into the sea. A monstrous wave must have swept the bay, for the bush that had come down to the water's edge had been flattened and swept away for half a mile inland.

True to its tradition, the Carima River gave up no dead—no bodies were ever found. Ezra made no attempt to search the fjord where the caves had been, for that work now needed skilled divers. He put the whole area under Army guard while I went back to London for technical help. Sir Edmund was in his element here—he knew precisely what to do, and who to go to, in both London and Washington, and a team of experts was rapidly assembled. They found the wreckage of the freighter, but with no bodies on board, and they found the remains of dynamos and various bits of what had been sophisticated electrical and radio equipment. The work of assessing it all was still going on.

A minesweeper, lent by the U.S. Navy, had been dispatched to sweep the area where the yacht had been blown up. She found two other mines. They were rudimentary affairs, made up of several forty-gallon oil drums, packed with high explosive in watertight wrappings, and lashed together. They had detonators which could have been fired by radio-control, but no effort seemed to have been made to prevent the mines from being set off by physical impact—carelessness, or the arrogance that comes from over-confidence, on someone's part. Rudimentary as they were, the mines were of devastating explosive power. The three of them would certainly have made a grand waterspout. One had been demonstrably enough to smash a 600-ton yacht to smithereens. The existence of the mines was not publicly disclosed.

The yacht herself had been chartered quite openly by a party of Chinese business men for a holiday trip from Jamaica to the islands. The Chinese Government rather pointedly expressed surprise at the apparent incompetence of American navigation, but otherwise took no interest in the matter. The body of the Chinese man picked up by the gunboat was never identified. He was buried in the big cemetery at Fort James. So was Nicolas Caval. There appeared to be no relatives to attend the funeral, and the Nuevan taxpayer paid.

The rest was speculation. We could never know why the young physicist had been killed—Ruth's guess that he was too honest for Charles's purposes was as good as any. What were Charles's purposes? To triumph after three centuries by getting hold of Edward Caval's lands? Nicolas Caval was apparently bankrupt. Li Cook, who was an astute business man, had been lending him money long before Nueva's independence, and held a mortgage on all his remaining property. Why Li Cook had not foreclosed remains a mystery. Presumably he felt that Nicolas Caval might be useful to him, and possibly Nicolas had argued that the best way for Li Cook to get paid was to ensure that Edward Caval's fortune should go to Nicolas. That, indeed, may have been the sordid beginning of the whole scheme, Li Cook's wider ambitions being awakened when he realised the international political importance of Charles's alleged invention.

My part in Li Cook's scheming was now obvious. The presence of a British officer in Nueva would give him an admirable excuse for discovering a plot for foreign intervention to justify his seizure of personal power. The real political dispute in Nueva over the development of tourism suited him splendidly. If I had been killed with Edward Caval when Chacarima House was destroyed, doubtless I should have been found responsible for causing the explosion. The murder of the young physicist and our discovery of the body forced his hand. He still didn't do badly—my arrest on a charge of plotting with the CIA while ostensibly on a British military mission to Nueva served two purposes at once, to whip up anti-British and anti-Amercian feelings to justify his own actions, and to get me out of the way. He must have been put out when my escape was reported to him. But not put out enough to change his own plans—or perhaps they had gone too far to be changed. Presumably he thought that I couldn't do much harm wandering in the Nuevan bush, or that the bush would soon dispose of me anyway. . . .

One of the nicer things about Sir Edmund Pusey is that he knows when not to interrupt a train of thought. But he had just given me a pleasant dinner, and I couldn't remain in a brown study for ever. I dragged myself back to his question. What was I going to do? I asked a question in my turn. "Is there still a job for me?"

"My dear Peter! You have covered yourself, and the Department, with glory. It's a pity that so few people will ever know about it—but the few who do are the people who matter in the world. We employ all sorts and conditions of men. Offhand, I can't think of any other millionaires at present on the payroll, but I don't see why I should hold that against you. I was thinking primarily about Ruth."

"I'm thinking about her, too. We both made disastrous marriages, hers worse than mine, for Sybil was no worse than thousands of other women who want a good time for themselves, whereas she found herself married to a brilliant psychopath—for Charles undoubtedly was brilliant, for all his warped and twisted personality. You have done a lot to help Ruth already."

"No more than she deserves. She is an outstanding mathematician, and with her peculiar knowledge of the mathematics

158

of earthquakes the chief scientists on both sides of the Atlantic are naturally on her doorstep. It was partly to protect her from them that I got her that Readership at Oxford. Only partly, though. Oxford's damned lucky to have her. Cambridge will be offering her a professorship before we know where we are. You'll have to stop that. She'll make Oxford world-famous in her special field of earth-wave mathematics. I was a little sad that she felt she had to go back to that rather third-rate university to serve out her notice."

"That was like Ruth. She keeps her bargains. She is due at Oxford tomorrow. She will like Oxford, I think. I shall have to go down to see her there."

"Peter, you come near to making me angry sometimes—in fact, you do make me angry. Have you absolutely no concern for her as a woman? Anyone can see that she is devoted to you."

"Of course I'm concerned about her as a woman. But I have to be careful, because our relationship is a strange one—already we are almost inextricably linked by our joint ownership of the Caval Estate. I have to see her on business. Sometimes I think there can be no future for either of us until we get rid of the lot. We have talked about this already, and we shall discuss it again."

"Why?"

"Well, take the Nuevan estates. Edward Caval was a kind of Roman patrician on the island. He was born and lived there, his family had been there for centuries. We're just absentee land-lords. We're thinking of making over most of the land to Nueva, though we'd both rather like to keep that nice old house at Naura-taka, to go there sometimes. And of course I'd like to keep the schooner."

"That still leaves you millionaires."

"I haven't finished. We thought we might found a new college at Oxford. Caval College. Old Edward would like that."

"And this is what you want to talk about when you go to see her in Oxford?"

"Yes."